GRIND HOUSE PRESS

WARNING

TRUE CRIME

SAMANTHA KOLESNIK

Grindhouse Press
PO BOX 521
Dayton, Ohio 45401

Grindhouse Press #058
ISBN-13: 978-1-941918-56-2

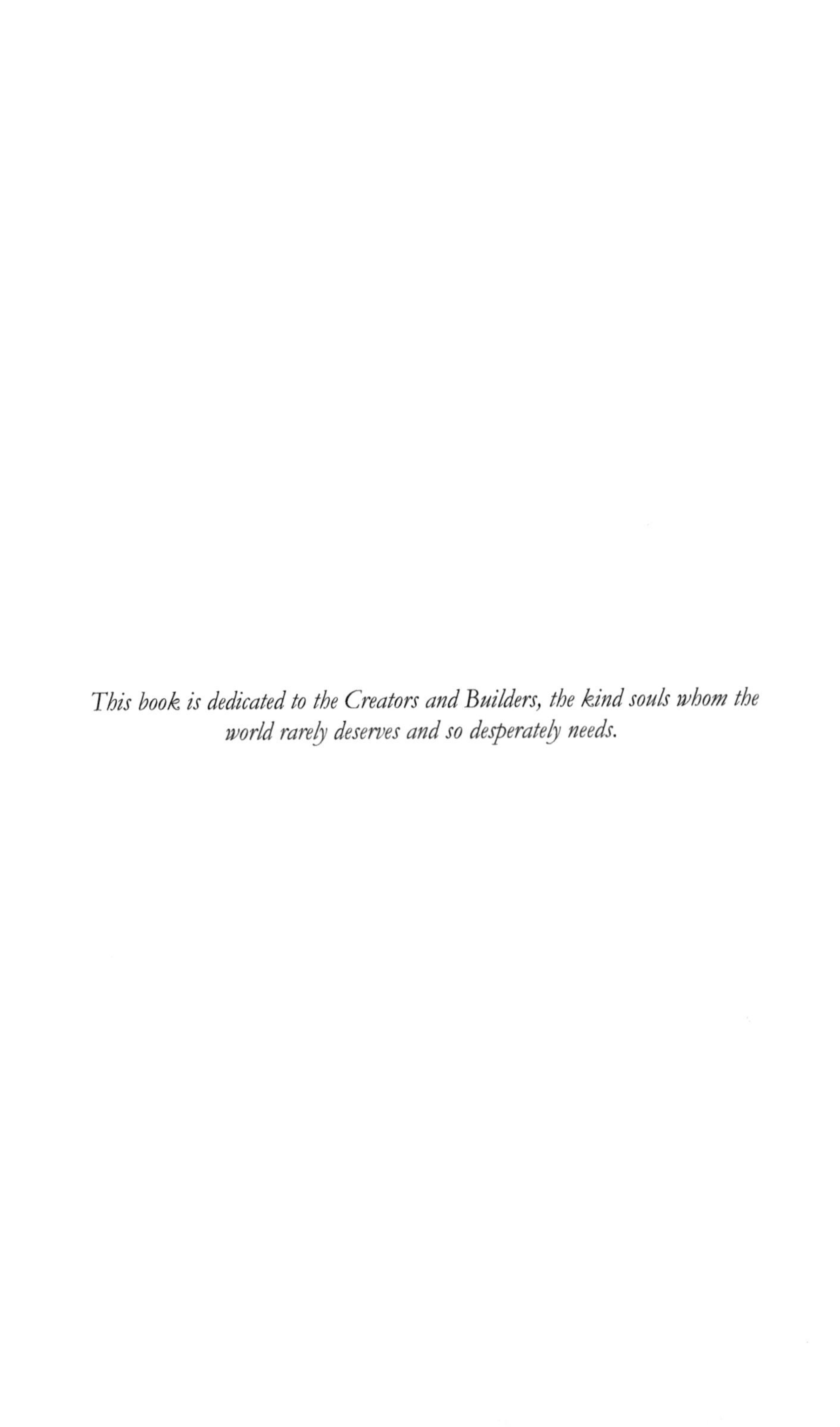

This book is dedicated to the Creators and Builders, the kind souls whom the world rarely deserves and so desperately needs.

1

I PULLED UP the piece of loose siding and slid out my best copy of *True Crime*. The pages, thin as newspaper, were gritty with dirt. I flipped to my favorite photo of a blonde murder victim from a few decades ago. The black ink had worn gray from my repeated touch. My obsessive fingers threatened to wipe away the entire page if given enough time.

The blonde in the photo had been babysitting when a man broke into the house and strangled her with an appliance cord. The photo left little to imagination and aroused an excitement in me—something similar, I imagined, to a young boy seeing his first centerfold. The blonde's lip was busted and her face was swollen. Her cheeks bulged unnaturally. The only living part was her hair, which fanned out around her head in a wild mess of blonde tangle.

TRUE CRIME

My brother, Lim, said I was sick. He said only sick people look at magazines like the one I held in my hands. I knew he was right; it wasn't normal.

The babysitter photo was the first time I'd seen a dead woman in the full. Usually *True Crime* cropped out the details. It'd show a pair of clogs and white socks drawn up over pale calves. It'd show legs splayed apart with just a tease of blood. There might be a hand flung out from behind a couch with a few bullet casings in the foreground.

There was no propriety with the babysitter, though. She was gold.

I didn't get a sexual thrill from looking at her. There was nothing climactic or conclusive about my obsession with her corpse. It just felt good.

When I had first seen the photo, I hadn't been able to look away for a long while. I had strained to scan every last detail of her into my memory. The recollection of it had become a prayer I could recount at times when my mind strained to escape Mama's very real and present hands.

Sometimes it helped if I imagined the scene in the photo from the man's point of view. I would try to feel the relief the man must have felt as he pulled on that cord around the blonde's tender neck. I imagined it must've been quite a bit of work to take away a woman's youth like that.

I put *True Crime* down and stared across the street.

Skinny Bart Tucker was breaking into the Clarksons' home in broad daylight. I leaned back on my elbows and watched the milky-skinned boy wrap a jacket around his fist and punch the glass panel by their front door. He reached inside, jiggled the lock, and walked right through.

A few minutes later, Bart came back out the front door carrying the Clarksons' flat-screen television set. His jeans slid lower and lower around his hips as he waddled across their crabgrass lawn.

He stopped in his tracks and looked across the street at me.

He yelled, "Hey! You're Lim's sister, right?"

I yelled back confirmation. Bart shook his head and kept waddling down the street in pants halfway past his ass, his colorful boxers showing like a flag of pride.

I leaned my head back on the iron porch rail and closed my eyes. The black iron felt hot in the summer heat. I lost track of time, drifting in and out of sleep, when Lim's large hand rocked my shoulder.

"Why are you outside all the time?" Lim asked.

I looked up at him. My brother was the closest thing most people could compare to a giant in real life. Lim was exceptionally tall and wide with a thinning pat of blond hair atop his head. His skin always looked buttery to me with its constant sweaty shimmer.

Lim's eyes were blue and cold. He never smiled with his eyes. It was only with his thin lips that he expressed joy—lips which appeared much too small in his large, round head.

People were scared of Lim. The only people I knew who didn't scare of Lim were me and Mama.

I shrugged him off and went for the front door. He was close behind. His shadow blocked out the sun. Before I opened the door, I slid my copy of *True Crime* into its hiding spot in the hole in the siding.

Mama was sitting on the couch inside. It was hard to avoid

looking at her. She was splayed out in oversized pink panties and an old sweatshirt she'd had since I was little. It was splattered with hair dye stains and filled me with bad memories.

Lim passed me and walked off down the adjacent hallway to his room. I was alone with the monster.

I tried to follow my brother's lead as I started for the hallway, but I felt her plotting against me as soon as my back was turned. It took everything I had not to play the dog. I braced myself for whatever would come next. My body was my mother's unfortunate toy.

"Where do you think you're going?" Mama asked in a low, cool tone.

Her calmness scared me. I preferred her when she was railing and going off the deep end about this or that. It was easier when she slammed things and yelled about how we didn't love her.

When she was calm, she liked to play games only she enjoyed.

"Come here," she said. Her tone was casual. She often didn't have to exert authority anymore. Truth was, I could play the dog well. My body knew from all the times she'd laid hands on it that if she told me to do something, she meant it.

I turned around and took a few steps closer to the couch.

"What's wrong?" I asked. My stomach soured. It was a sickness particular to me and Mama. It was something we would always share.

If the sickness came when she was not with me, which it did during the night and at school, especially in the gym auditorium where I saw glimpses of other girls' legs, I felt her. I felt Mama. Other kids went to the school nurse because they were sad about their grades or had a runny nose.

My sickness was different. And I never went to the school nurse.

"Take off that shirt," Mama said.

"I don't want to." I looked at the ground. I was wearing a lime green tank top without a bra. I regretted it because I could feel her eyes on my breasts, which had grown to a B cup in the past three months.

"Come on, Suzy, take it off. We're both women," she said.

I closed my eyes and thought of the babysitter in the photo. I tried hard to imagine what it had felt like for the man to have stared into that young girl's eyes as he squeezed her airway shut. I often wondered, "What does a woman look like the moment she dies? What does life leaving really leave?"

"Go on," Mama said. I heard one of her small moans. They were ugly noises she reserved for our time together. I didn't have to look at her; I knew what she was doing.

I slid off my top and tossed it on the floor. The exposure shocked my breasts and made them feel tender. They reacted in a way I didn't want them to and I felt embarrassed for it. I crossed my arms and tried to hide myself.

I looked at Mama. She had one hand on her crotch and the other propping her head up. Her eyes were right on my breasts. Framing her red face was her unruly mess of hair.

I hated those hairs. I hated finding them everywhere around the house. I hated cleaning them up with the mildew in the bathtub.

"Don't hide them. What are you hiding them for?" she said.

I dropped my arms and let her look. I disliked my breasts because they were about as big as hers now. Sometimes boys at school looked at them and I wondered if they could see what had been done to them. What had been done to me.

Other girls talked about how they wanted their breasts to be bigger and all I wanted to do was cut mine off.

I bent down to pick up my tank top, but Mama halted me with an upraised hand.

"Lim!" she yelled.

"Mama, no . . ." I pleaded.

"Lim!" she yelled again. Her eyes were aflame with excitement. I wanted to scream, but I knew it would arouse her all the more. I remained quiet and ashamed. It was better to obey because then it would be over quicker.

Lim shuffled out of the hallway. He took in the room's horrors, but his expression never changed from its placid, fixed position. Lim was calm in chaos.

"Look at your sister's tits."

My face was hot. I wanted to run, but she'd come catch me and I'd be worse for it.

Lim didn't immediately comply.

"I said look at your sister's tits," she repeated.

Lim finally took a look. I met his eyes briefly as they shifted upward from my exposed chest but saw nothing in his gaze. He looked empty.

"Aren't they getting big?" she goaded.

"I've seen bigger," Lim said with a shrug.

Our mother sneered. I could feel her dissatisfaction. I wondered if Lim felt it, too. She turned back to the television with her hand still deep in her panties. I saw a swath of her dark curly pubic hair and felt like throwing up.

2

I AWOKE IN the middle of the night. My stomach was sour, its contents threatening to show themselves. The nightmare from which I'd awoken was too sickening to rehash. I put a hand between my legs and felt the place I never wanted to feel. I felt her fingers there so often that my own felt foreign.

Sleeping was as dangerous as waking. There was no way to escape my mother.

I pulled at the drapes next to my bed and looked out into the starless sky. Poetry always talked about the sky and its innumerable stars. But there were no stars in Morris Grove.

I took advantage of the permissive nature of darkness and allowed myself to cry. I knew better than to cry in front of others. If I did that, I'd get hurt. One time, I got hurt bad for it.

I called out into the darkness, "Alice, are you there?"

Alice was a young girl Mama had kidnapped and kept locked in the basement. I could secretly talk to her through the vent in my bedroom. She was a comfort to me. Besides Lim and me, Alice was the only one who knew what it was like to be with my mother.

"I don't want her to hurt us anymore," I whispered through the floor. The only response was the faintest clattering of her chain.

When I thought of Alice, I thought of a crime story that really got to me once. It was about a young girl who was left in the care of her parents' neighbor and ended up getting tortured like an animal. Words were carved into her flesh. When I read about that one, my skin lit on fire with rage. No one saved her. The girl died dehumanized like an animal tortured for the thrill.

And the hag that did it all to her? I think she was even set free.

"We're not going to let Mama get away with this," I assured Alice.

I turned away from the window and I lay back down in my bed. On the brink of sleep, I thought of Moses:

I was five when Mama brought Moses home. He was a Scottish Terrier puppy. The happiness I felt when I first saw him has never been surpassed.

When I showed the puppy to my brother, his face looked dark. I couldn't understand why he wasn't excited.

Moses and I were very close. I told him secrets. He licked my face when I was sad. Lim said that was kind of gross, but I didn't mind it. When I was around Moses, it felt like even I could be loved by something.

When those happy times ended with Moses, so did the last of my childhood.

It was with Moses that Mama broke me.

I was always bad according to Mama. I tried everything I could to change, but nothing I did raised my value in her eyes. And one day, she thought I was so bad she said Moses was going to be punished.

I told her it wasn't Moses that was bad. It was me.

The fear I felt that day left scars only I can see. She towered over me when I stood up for Moses. I cried because I thought she was going to hit me again.

Mama hated it when I cried. She told me if I kept crying, Moses would never eat again. I still hate myself for it, but I just couldn't stop. I held the tears in for as long as I could but when I lost control of my bladder, the tears came pouring out.

It was my badness again.

I could play with Moses, Mama said, but we weren't allowed to give him any food. As the days passed, Moses changed into a different kind of animal. His body thinned and mucous formed around his eyes.

He didn't lick my face anymore; he didn't even lick his own nose.

Then one night, Lim slipped through the shadows of my bedroom. He had Moses swaddled in his arms.

We snuck out the back porch with the puppy in tow. I held him in my arms and felt his ribcage softly pulse with shallow breaths.

I told him I was sorry.

Lim looked into my eyes. I saw something behind his cold gaze. It wasn't love, but it reassured me. He said, "Suzy, it's better this way."

And then Lim hugged me and he made a noise that might've been a sob, but it sounded more like the sudden and guttural cry of an animal in pain. He held me so tight, I thought he might crush me and Moses both.

He whispered into my ear words I've not since forgotten. He said, "You can always trust me, Suzy."

Lim saw to it that night that Moses didn't suffer anymore.

My friend at school said Moses had gone to doggy heaven. I was only five, but I was smart enough to know there was no place like that.

3

I STAYED OUTSIDE as often as I could when Lim wasn't home. Mama got mad when I wandered off alone too far from the neighborhood. She said something bad might happen to me. So I hung around close to the house, just not inside it.

It could have been worse. I could have been like Alice, who was trapped in the darkness and confined to a chain. Seasons no longer existed for Alice.

The grass tickled. I wore a sundress the local Baptist church donated to us from their "One Community" program. It was yellow with a bird pattern embroidered in a swoop across the skirt. I didn't want to let on that I loved it, so I wore it very rarely.

As I relaxed in the sun, I thought about Alice. I imagined us running around at a fair where we could chase each other between games and rides. I'd catch a goldfish for us both and we'd eat cotton candy until our fingers were coated in the crystallized sugar. Alice had read the book *Charlotte's Web* and told me if she ever got out of Mama's basement, she would buy a prize pig for herself and would name him Wilbur like in the book. Alice said there were spiders in the basement just like there were in the book. She had told me through the vent one night she'd begun to welcome their company. The touch of anything living gave her hope, or so she said.

I thought of Moses, too. I skimmed my hand over the grass petals and tried to speak to him through the power of my mind. I'd read once on a door mailer that I needed to let God into my heart and pray for his forgiveness.

That never worked for me. Any time I tried to talk to God, it just sounded like my own thoughts. Perhaps the part of my brain meant for talking with God was broken or deformed. Maybe when God created me, he disliked his creation and turned off the part connecting me to him, like an artist who didn't want to sign a bad painting.

If it were different, then I would ask God to have Moses back. I'd ask God to let Moses be big and strong so he could eat my enemies.

And Alice—she'd have her prize pig and we'd travel the country showing him off. Alice told me her mom had taught her how to knit, so maybe we'd knit the pig little piggy clothes. We'd make him a real attraction like Wilbur was in the book. We wouldn't even need jobs because we'd have a show pig.

A cold chill came over me. It was the spreading shadow of another taking me over.

I looked up and saw Dean, Mama's on-again, off-again boyfriend. His gold-toothed grin glinted in the sunlight. His face was ruddy with the evidence of hard labor.

"You look good," Dean said. He spat after he said it. The glob of his saliva landed on the edge of one of the pretty embroidered birds on my dress. I scurried out from under his shadow, but even the sun didn't feel so warm anymore.

Dean cocked his head and let out a whistle. He, too, expected me to play the dog.

"Your mom's short on the rent again. I said you could help a little. Like last time," he said.

As I followed Dean into the house, I thought once more of Alice. I imagined her running in front of me and tossing smiles over her shoulder. I tried to envision the specifics of her features. I wondered what the curve of her collarbone was like and the angle of her nose. I wondered at the tint of her eyes and how her face might look when she smiled. I wondered if she'd ever smile again.

Mama waited for me in the living room in a too-tight negligee. It was a real awful slip of a thing that looked like the washer had worked it over one too many times. She threw a wad of lace at me. I opened up the garment and could see it was an awful thing with cloth missing in all the places where it was needed most.

"Put it on," she said.

I looked around for Lim, but I already knew he wasn't there. I had the instinct to seek him out in all my times of need and to hope his strong, meaty hand would reach out in protection.

The only people with me were Mama and Dean. And there was

the blonde babysitter; she stared out from the void of my memory's secret depths. I imagined my hands gripping her throat.

"This ain't gonna work, Sherry. Look at her. She's scared stupid. Why don't I give her something to loosen her up?" Dean said, as if I were dumb and deaf. As if I couldn't hear him standing right there.

But dogs didn't have conversations. Dogs only obeyed.

"Oh it's going to work," Mama said. "Come here."

I walked over to Mama. She undid my favorite sundress, snapping the buttons one by one. She relished each pop; she took her time disrobing me.

The air was electric. The hairs on my arms stood on end and something pulled me up and out of that place.

I thought of my first day at kindergarten. The teacher took the class out to recess. The other kids were laughing and running everywhere. There was so much noise and laughter. It was stressful. Some children lined up for the slide; others played on the tire swing. I had stood paralyzed on the sidelines. I didn't know how to play like them.

I often left my body and lost track of the time. My imagination took me places when my body had to endure things my mind couldn't. My flesh was a monument to bad things I wished I could forget. I wondered if that was what people meant when they said they felt God in their hearts because what happened was not of me. I was not what I did. And I was not what was done unto me.

I thought of the children hopping from one chalk-drawn square to the next . . .

. . . and I thought of them dangling from the monkey bars, the hot metal clenched in their small hands.

Hands.

Her hands.

On my back and rubbing, sliding lower to undo the last buttons.

The ash fell through my fingers and the cigarettes launched through the air. I pushed Mama back on the couch. I grabbed one of her breasts; it was just something to hold onto. I slammed the glass ashtray against her head with an uneven and rapid rhythm. My assault was unflagging.

Her arms scratched and pushed, but this only made me squeeze her breast harder, as if I had to hold on or else lose my power.

I slammed her head again. I felt her hands on me, at my neck and at my sundress, which hung limply around my hips. I was half naked but that didn't matter. The only thought I had was for her to stop moving.

Her stillness became the twinkle in my eye.

It was not pleasant to beat her. After a time, she could only twitch and I hoped she'd stop moving altogether because my arm had tired and my grip was weak.

When I was done with my mother, her breast was black and blue, and her head was red and black. I'd made something of her after all.

I turned around expecting to see Dean. I was scared I'd have to fight him, too. The God feeling was gone and I didn't think I could do what I did all over again.

But Dean was gone. All he left was a lonesome belt on the ground and an open door through which a warm breeze wafted through the house.

Mama's blood soured in the heat.

4

"JESUS, SUZY, SHE'S still breathing," Lim said.

If Mama could see herself, she'd be pretty angry, because she had bled all over the couch. You couldn't clean a mess like that.

Lim paced back and forth across the living room. Every few moments, Mama reached out a hand toward her son. Her eyes bulged. Her tongue attempted speech, but English was no longer possible.

"How long ago was Dean here?" Lim asked for the third time.

I shrugged. After I'd done up Mama like I did, I'd lost all sense of time. It could have been hours since Dean had left, but it could just as well have been minutes.

I poked my head through the drapes and saw that dusk had settled in. "I guess it was a few hours," I said.

Lim grabbed my shoulders in his thick hands. He roughly turned me and I couldn't help looking into his cold, worriless eyes which belied the grave tone in which he addressed me.

"Suzy, you're in a lot of trouble. You know that?"

My eyes darted around the room. It was plain to me what a man needed to do in this situation—as plain as the images I obsessed over—images memorialized in black and white newspaper print.

I shrugged myself out of Lim's grip. I went and detached the ironing board cord. Mama grew restless. She could see me doing it.

I handed Lim the cord. It was thick and strong. A man with hands like Lim's could work miracles with a cord like that.

I rested next to Mama for a moment. I ran my fingers through her bloody hair and decided I liked her hair better that way. The blood took all the frizz out.

"You're crazy, Suzy," Lim muttered. He stared at the cord in his hands.

"We're crazy, Lim. We're all crazy." I patted Mama's head. Her eyes swiveled in her skull so they could look right at me. They were still unkind.

"Do you remember, Lim," I started in, "when we were little, and Mama would have us go collect the bottles from the highway?"

Lim nodded, twisting and playing with the cord in his hands.

"And do you remember, I had gotten a little ahead of you? And that guy had drove up, in his nasty car, and he tried to get me to go with him. Do you remember what you did that day?"

Lim took a step closer to me and Mama. I could have sworn his gaze softened, but I could have sworn the sky was red, too, and I also could have sworn that Alice was listening through the cobwebbed air ducts from the basement.

I laughed a little, but I might have also cried. I said, "And when the neighborhood boys saw him, they knew who did it. And you know, no one messed with me after that. Sometimes one would try but the others would stop them. They would always say, 'Aren't you Lim's sister?' And that was all it took."

"This isn't Moses, Suzy," Lim said as he approached our mother.

It wasn't as interesting as I thought it would be when he wrapped the cord around her neck. She was so weak she barely fought. Her fingers barely touched the cord and then they fell after a short time. Her face became too many colors and her tongue swelled. When she stopped breathing, I couldn't help but think, "*That's all?*"

Lim went out to the garage and returned with two gasoline cans. I rummaged through Mama's purse and pulled out the little cash I could find, a gas station credit card, and some old movie ticket coupons.

I liked the movies.

I grabbed one can and Lim grabbed the other. We zig-zagged throughout the house and soon the smell of fuel overtook blood's foul and coppery stench.

"Take a change of clothes out to the car and I'll be right out," Lim said. I ran to my bedroom and stuffed a few things in my backpack. Not much was worth keeping.

Night had settled on Morris Grove. I sat in the passenger seat and waited for Lim. My backpack was tucked between my legs. I spat on a napkin and tried to rub off some of the blood on my face.

Lim hurried out the front door. Just as he reached the car, I saw a glow from behind the living room drapes. My eyes lingered on the house as the engine revved. Something shadowy stared at me from the basement window.

As we took off, I craned my head and tried to make out the shadow in the basement, but soon it faded both from my gaze and from my thoughts.

The whole house was going to burn down and I guessed that whatever—whomever—was inside, they were going to burn, too. Traveling pigs and puppies, God and Moses, those were all dreams, just the same. Only crime was true.

5

I HAD A tickle in my ear that first night alone with Lim on the road. It was like a bug crawled in and wouldn't stop trying to get his way out of there. I stuck my finger in and clawed out some wax. There was no bug.

Lim minded the speed limit, but I still tensed up every time we passed a parked cruiser. As anxious as I felt, there was a real preciousness to what we had done.

I flipped down the mirror and tried to see myself through another's eyes. If it weren't still a secret, what we'd done, my eyes would be cold on every newspaper front page. Moms and Dads would look at me and Lim and they wouldn't see any difference from famous killers.

We had crossed that sacred line into the realm of men who killed, and not on anyone's authority but our own. We were a part of an exclusive underground club of travelers winding their way throughout the United States highways, blood drying on their hands.

I didn't take a special joy in the fact that I had killed. Did the trash man take joy in his haul? It was something that needed doing.

"Are you gonna drive all night?" I asked Lim.

"As far as I can," he said.

"Where are we gonna sleep?"

"Should've thought of that before you smashed her damn head open."

Lim punched the radio knob and those old 80s songs played one after the next. They were the kind of songs that played in those films with the red-headed freckled girl who was always trying to get a boyfriend.

Molly Ringer. Molly Rigson. Something like that.

I loved the movies. I rolled my window down and let the summer air blow me back. I mimed bringing a cigarette to my lips. I took the inhale and everything.

My thoughts raced with images of all my favorite tough guys in the movies—Perry from *The Wanderers*, Dallas from *The Outsiders*, Tony from *Scarface*—I loved all those guys. I wanted to be them.

There was never a woman who I wanted to be. The movies didn't show any women worth emulating. Just lumps and mounds, colors and shapes. Heaps of flesh you could make into chaos.

I sucked my imaginary cigarette down to its nub and flicked it out the window like a tough guy would.

I looked at my hands—so small and soft. Lim said women's

hands felt like tissue. I slumped against the side door and thought about old-fashioned dance halls, the kinds I'd seen in movies. The men came home from the war and the women huddled in their dresses whispering about the men.

There was always one woman who didn't know what she wanted in those kinds of movies. The man would go to her and ask for her hand. Would any man want to hold my hand, a hand that killed? Would I want him to?

I thought about men and hands, dances and women's shapes, as I fell asleep.

When morning came, it came with a visitor.

6

SOMEONE RAPPED THE window by Lim. I opened my eyes and saw the butt of a rifle tapping against the glass—*rat tat tat*—and so on. All I saw at first was a flannel shirt tucked neatly into brass-buckled jeans. The hand holding the gun was wrinkled and tanned.

I pinched Lim's arm hard. He sprung awake and looked like he was about to hit me before his senses came to him.

"Who the hell is that?" Lim muttered.

I looked out the window to my right. We were parked in a ditch beside endless rows of corn. I couldn't see over the stalks in my direction, but through the windshield I saw a long stretch of road and not much else. Just one stripe of pavement cutting through.

"You think we should just get on?" Lim asked.

The rifleman popped a squat outside Lim's window. He wore a beige cowboy hat, the brim brought so low it rested on his bushy white eyebrows. He stared right at us in a way that could not be ignored.

"See what he wants," I said.

Lim rolled down the window and eyed the cowboy.

"Y'all parked in my corn field," the old man said.

"Needed to take a rest," Lim said.

The old man poked his head in the car and gave me a good once over. I felt his eyes linger on my growing chest. I wondered if he had a good butcher knife, being a farm man and all.

"That your girl?" the old man asked.

Lim gave me a look, but his eyes were imperceptibly cold.

"Yeah, I'm his," I said. I figured the longer we waited to answer, the sooner we'd be in trouble.

"Well where the heck y'all headed that got you's out here in Hansen?" asked the old man. He propped himself up on his long rifle and waited with some kind of authority, as if he were owed an explanation. I guessed these farm men felt they were kings of their land. They were arbiters of all that was 'right' and 'needed' because they planted some seeds and poured their sweat into the ground. I didn't see anything that special about a farm.

Lim slumped in his seat a little. He could be slow on the uptake.

"Well," he began, stumbling through a lie, "I lost my job and I don't really know where we're headed." Lim shrugged his broad, meaty shoulders and looked out over the road.

"He's a good worker," I said and patted Lim's shoulder like I was showing off a prized workhorse.

The old cowboy wheezed a heavy sigh and dipped into his pocket. He pulled out a small tin of chewing tobacco and let into it. Soon he was talking around a lump under his bottom lip. His tongue darted between his lips like a dog licking shit.

"I got some work you can do, but—" and he paused there. I saw his eyes catch my breasts again and I wondered about that knife.

"But you's ain't married?" the old man finished asking in one foul breath.

Lim shook his head.

"Then you's can't be sleeping together no-how in my house."

The old man spat tobacco-brown. A few specks of his spittle decorated our windshield.

"Your girl can sleep with mine. I got a granddaughter, Lena."

"That sounds fine," I said, surprised at how mild and sweet my voice sounded.

"Keep on this road a quarter mile up. You'll see a dirt road to the right. Sharp right. Keep on that till you hit the farmhouse. You won't miss it. Park yer car anywhere you like. Tell Lena to cook you up something. I'll be around in a bit."

The cowboy spat again and pointed his rifle on down the road.

"Thattaway now. Get on."

Lim straightened his seat and turned on the engine. We rolled slowly down the road.

"Should we just keep on?" Lim asked.

"We need money and we need food," I reminded him.

"I don't like the way he was looking at you," Lim mentioned. I looked at his face. I hoped to see an emotion or concern, but all I saw was flesh.

"There's the road." I pointed at a dirt road that drew a sharp line through the corn crop.

Lim pulled the car to a stop. "Yeah, there it is. But you sure?"

Lim ran his hand over his pat of buttery hair. His cheeks glistened with sweat. "We can keep on. We don't have to stop here."

"I don't know. I'm hungry," I lied. Truth was, I didn't have much of an appetite and I didn't really care about the money, though I knew we'd need it. What I really wanted was to see if they had pigs like in *Charlotte's Web* and if there was one of those big butcher houses. I never saw something properly gutted and I wanted to.

"Alright," Lim sighed. He turned down the dirt road and eased on at a crawl. The corn stalk leaves scraped against the car as we moseyed along. It seemed like as good a place as any to hide.

The farmhouse was two stories of wood with chipped and peeling paint. There was a barn next to it and, in the distance, a small grazing pen with skinny cows. I didn't see any pigs right off.

A young woman, maybe a few years older than me, hung some sheets on the line outside. She startled when she heard us pull up.

Lim ducked his head out the window. "We came from your granddad. He said he's got some work for me. Said to ask you to cook something."

I added, "If it isn't much trouble."

I stepped out of the car. My feet hit the ground for the first time since leaving Mama. It felt so good to stretch my legs. Gnats circled my head, but even they felt kind of good. Their nibbles reminded me

I was alive.

"I'm Alice," I said. "And that's my brother, Mick."

Lim looked at me and mouthed the word, "Mick?"

The woman took a few steps closer. I drank her in. She was lean except for a small bulge in her belly where I noticed she kept putting her hand as if she were making sure the bulge was still there. She was pregnant. Her blonde hair was close to her shoulders and shoved back with a kerchief. As she neared to me, I could see her skin wasn't soft like tissue, like Lim said. Someone had put her to work or had worked her over. I couldn't decide.

"I'm Lena," she said with a nod at me and my brother. "We can't spare much, but I can cook up some eggs if that's alright."

"We're sorry to put you out." I smiled. I wanted to reach out and feel her hair. I wanted to run my fingers through the grit and try to find the bugs. She looked like she would be lousy.

We followed Lena to the house. She pulled back the battered screen door for us. We walked into the living room right onto the old, creaky floor planks. The air was thick inside. It was hard to breathe.

"There's a breeze in the kitchen if you's want to come in here," Lena said. We followed her into the kitchen. It smelled like grease and tobacco.

Lim and I sat down at an old puff-top square table. The chairs had torn foam seats with bits of yellow flesh oozing from the stained plastic covers. I didn't feel much of a breeze, but I took her word that it'd come.

I watched Lena dip a towel into Crisco and smear the white grease around the skillet.

"Where you's all from that you ended up in Hansen?" she wondered. "Nobody ever comes by here."

"We're from the south," I said.

"This is the south," Lena said. She ticked on the gas stove and a pyramid of blue light appeared over the burner. Those gas stoves always put me on edge.

"You know, the south-south," I said.

"The south-south," Lena repeated. She cracked one egg after the other right into the skillet. They sizzled.

"How long have you and your granddad lived here?" I asked.

Lena laughed without humor. "You can't tell from the looks of it? Since forever." She brushed the pile of egg shells into her shirt and dumped them in the trash can. "We'll probably die with this place."

"You don't sound too happy about that," I reckoned.

Lim's cold eyes shot a warning at me.

Lena shook the skillet.

"Nobody's happy in Hansen," she said grimly. I watched her put her hand back on her swollen belly.

I heard the screen door open and soon the old man was upon us, his face dripping sweat. He smelled of something awful.

"Just in time," Lena said. She took a few plates off the drying rack and slid a fried egg each onto them.

"Thought I smelled something cookin'," the old man said. He took his egg standing up and ate it with his hands. The bulbous yolk split in his mouth. It ran its yellow juices down his chin and onto his fingers, which he sucked on without shame. As he sucked up every last yellow drop, his eyes lingered on my chest. It ruined what little appetite I had.

Lim ate his portion quickly. I moved my egg around on my plate. Every time I swished it from one side to the other, the yolk jiggled like a blob of fat. It was strange to think this egg could have turned out to be a chicken.

"You ever get eggs that are full of blood?" I asked.

Lim shot me another look, "What are you going on about?"

"My Mama," and I blanched when I said her name because I could feel Lim's eyes bore into my skull. "My Mama said sometimes the eggs are full of blood, with little baby chickens inside."

The cowboy laughed. He shared a look with Lim, or at least he tried to. It was one of those exchanges men made without talking. They always said the same thing, those exchanges. "Ain't them women silly," the cowboy's eyes said.

"You should eat and stop thinkin' so much," the old man said.

Lena gave a second thought to Lim. She leaned down to take his plate, "You want somethin' else?"

Lim looked at the old man in another private exchange. Men always treaded carefully around each other's women. I made it easy on them both and slid my plate to Lim, "Here. Have mine."

The cowboy stood there for a moment. I watched him watch us both with different sets of eyes. He saw two different animals before him. He thought to tame one, and with the other, I didn't know yet. But I had my suspicions.

I looked at Lena's belly then, and upward my eyes traveled to her swarthy-skinned face and sad little eyes.

7

THE DAY WAS early yet. I helped Lena finish hanging the wash. I pinned up a pair of her panties. They were pink with yellow flowers on them. They looked like a girl's. I was embarrassed to look at them, but when I looked at Lena, she didn't seem to care at all.

The cowboy had taken Lim off to do some work in the fields. I was glad to be free of the old man.

"You don't have to help me if you don't want," Lena said.

"I want to," I said. She looked at me like a child looked at an animal in a zoo. I realized I was smiling at her and I started to blush. I felt Mama's hand inside of me and it made my skin squirm. All I could do was look away.

I counted corn stalks in a row until the feeling lessened.

"That was funny back there, what you asked," Lena said. She walked over so she was right in front of me. She wiped her hands on her shirt but, even so, I could see she was dirty. "About them eggs and blood."

"Yeah, it was pretty stupid, I guess," I said.

"No, I thought about it once, too," she confessed. Lena put two hands on her belly then, unaware of herself. "We take their children, kill them, right? Eat them, too. And no one cares."

"You think they have feelings?" I asked.

She spat on the ground. "You think them men think us women have feelings? You got a heart that beats, you got feelings, Alice. And every daughter on this earth is just somebody's broodmare."

Lena stalked off into the house. I looked at her butt as she left. It was small and lean, almost like a boy's. There wasn't much to her except for that belly she rubbed. I wished I could look like that. With every step I took after her, I felt my butt move from side to side. My growing breasts jiggled up and down. In every place where I wanted to be hard and small, I was soft and growing.

I wished someone would take a knife to me and treat me like a chicken. I wished they'd cut off my parts and package them to be sold. I didn't need them.

I found Lena in the kitchen. She stood over the sink, running water into a pail. The pail soon overflowed and the water splashed over the sides. Her shoulders hunched and her body shivered. She was crying.

I walked toward her with careful step by careful step. Her sobs, so dark in the bright noontime sun, fascinated me. I didn't want them to stop. I wanted to touch her. I wanted her to know I knew how that was—to cry so hard and long and without anyone to share your pain.

I raised my hand to her back and let my fingers hover by the nape of her neck. I listened to her try to console herself. She tried to swallow her own cries.

Lena looked at me sideways. Her eyes were puffy. Her face glistened with tear streaks.

"I don't want it, you know?" she said.

I leaned against the counter and watched her. I let her talk.

"I don't want this." She clutched at her belly. She grabbed at it like she was trying to yank something out of her. "Not here, anyhow."

"Is it his?" I asked.

"Granddad's?" Lena rolled her eyes. She turned off the water and heaved the pail out of the sink. Water splashed over both our shoes. "You must think we're really backward, huh?"

I shrugged. "I don't see anyone else here is all."

"It's not his," Lena said and she looked at me with a meanness I hadn't realized was in her.

"You need help?" I asked.

"No," she said flatly and walked off with her water pail, not bothering to keep much water in it as it sloshed from side to side.

I decided to let her be.

8

THE SUN KISSED the horizon. I kicked up dust around the house and moseyed along to the cow pen.

There were five skinny brown cows in the pen with one paler than all the rest. As I unlatched the gate, my hand caught a splinter from the gnarled wood. I looked at the thin black sliver in the crest of my palm. It was so little compared to what my hands had done.

I walked over to the pale cow. The animal's ribs jutted out from beneath her velvety skin. I laid my hand on her side and felt along her ribcage. She didn't move at my touch.

It was weird to think things like ice cream came from these animals. The pale beast looked at me. Her eyes warbled around in her head like she was trying to say something. It felt pleading.

It struck me then how much distance we put between ourselves and animals. Perhaps this was from design, to ensure the very thin line which kept us polite would seem thick and impenetrable. We were all murderers, after all. Some of us just hadn't discovered it yet.

I bent down and looked her straight in the eye. I stared at her for a while. Flies indiscriminately landed on us both and we selflessly fed them.

It occurred to me then that maybe I'd missed something of an opportunity. I put my hand on the cow's neck and closed my eyes. I thought back to Mama on the couch with her head all a rainbow. Lim and I just left her there. We left everything.

There with that pale cow on the farm—with dirt under my nails and close to nature—I wondered if we should've taken a piece of Mama with us.

It was too late now.

I thought about killing that pale cow. I wondered how Lena and the old man butchered them. Maybe in the barn.

I kicked around the pen, taking idle joy in watching bursts of dust bloom beneath my skidding shoes. The other cows were different; they steered clear of me. I came to realize cows were docile creatures and therefore it didn't surprise me men killed them in droves.

And it didn't surprise me there probably wasn't any joy in it.

I sat in the middle of the cow pen. The beasts, with the exception of the pale one, shuffled around me until they were all a comfortable distance from where I sat. The pale cow stood her ground a foot away, her formerly roving eyes now still and sad. A fly landed on one of them and still she didn't blink. I couldn't tell her apart from death itself.

I took up a big stick and started digging around like I had when I was a kid. Before we lived in Morris Grove we'd lived in some other park and the yard was nothing but sand. I used to dig in the backyard in the summertime out of boredom. Lim had told me that if I dug far enough, I'd reach China and I'd stupidly believed it.

Now I got to about a foot or so deep when I saw something strange jutting out from the dirt in the hole. I leaned down close enough to smell the scent of the earth. It smelled foul, like ripened garbage.

It was hair. It looked like dark hair. I used my hands to dig deeper. The mud caked up thick under my nails and stained my skin. There was something hard, like a huge rock.

And then I felt a shadow come over me. I turned around and saw Lena staring down at me.

"You gonna tell?" she asked.

I shook my head.

The gnats were thick and the sun was slim to none at this point.

"Here, get it covered," she said and started kicking the dirt I'd dug up back into the hole. I stood and helped her. After we'd filled it back up, we both stomped around on it like we were doing a perverse jig.

We locked eyes. Her dark tan looked like deep gold in the dim light of dusk. It had a dewy sheen to it.

Lena grabbed my hand and pulled me close to her.

She whispered, "You can't tell no one. Please."

I stared back at her.

"Here." She tugged on my arm. Lena led me out beyond the

house, up a hill, and into a stretch of meadow. It was almost dark but I could make out the field of tall, dry grass. Their tassels pricked and scratched my skin as we walked.

"Watch out for ticks," she said, as we walked farther and farther into the field.

I looked back at the house and saw a light on in the kitchen. The yellow light illuminated a small space inside, but I didn't see anyone there. Not the old man and not Lim.

Lena, ahead of me, became a dark shifting shape leading into further darkness. I had a strange feeling of foreboding. I felt like I was playing the dog again and I looked around to see who was holding the leash. It felt like Mama had her hands on me again.

"Lena," I called out.

"Hang on," she said. We'd reached a tree line. I swiveled my head around and saw the farmhouse was just an outline in the distance—two yellow spots like eyes staring out.

"You're real sweet," Lena said. "You and your brother," she continued. She'd given up the goat. Everyone called you sweet before they defiled you. A virgin was nothing if not ripe for the teeth.

It was dark now—too dark to see where Lena was. I sank into the grass and pushed back on my heels. I made myself as still as a dead girl.

I heard something then. Like metal scraping across rock.

"Alice," she said, "where'd you go?"

I didn't move.

"I didn't realize how dark it was getting," Lena said. She was trying to be quiet where she stepped. She was on the move.

"He wasn't a nice man," she continued. "I was young when it started."

Her footsteps were getting closer. The meadow grass swished and swayed around me. My heart didn't change its slow pace, but my face felt adrenaline's flush.

I wondered what Lena planned to do with me. Maybe she would grind me up and feed me to that skinny pale cow. I saw its roving looney eyes in the darkness. It had seen me alright.

"You wouldn't know what it's like," she spat. Her voice hardened. "Granddad caught him once on me and he told him he'd kill him if it happened again, but it never stopped. Granddad would have to leave and it'd be me and him. The things he'd do to me, Alice." Her voice cracked. "The things he'd do."

All of nature began to hum along with her refrain, echoing her pain.

The things he'd do, the flies buzzed.

The things he'd do, the snakes hissed.

The things he'd do, the frogs croaked.

All men did was rape, kill, eat, and fuck, as far as I could see, and it's not like the fields knew any different. The world was just an echo chamber for man's sin.

I lost myself in the hum of suffering when she came upon me. I felt and heard her footsteps. They were soft against the grass. The ground softened and cracked under her light steps. She was gentle with it.

"I'm sorry," she said. I looked up at her and saw a beast within a beast. She raised a shovel far above her head—outlined by the moonlight—and the giant behind her wrapped his thick hands around her throat. He lifted her into the air as her legs kicked out from beneath her. The shovel dropped with a thud.

Lim hung onto her in his grip. Her limbs wiggled and wobbled like one of those dolls on strings. I looked up at the sky to see if maybe anyone was holding the sticks.

Lim dropped Lena to the ground. She was pretty still, but I took the shovel all the same.

I didn't want to hurt her. But I didn't want her to breathe or talk, either. So I lifted the shovel up and swung it down. I repeated this like an exercise until my muscles couldn't handle it any longer.

Metal made quick work of bone and flesh.

"She has a baby inside her," I said when all was said and done.

Lim nodded.

"Do you think it's still breathing?" I asked. I bent down and turned her over. I put my hand on the soft bulge. I didn't feel anything. I put my ear down to her stomach to see if I could hear the baby.

"I don't hear a thing," I said. Lim stared down at Lena. His eyes were a mystery—a mystery I thought I saw crying in the moonlight.

I followed Lim back through the fields to the farmhouse. We passed those same skinny cows along the way.

"Hang on," he said once we got close enough to see each other through the light in the farmhouse windows.

"For what?" I asked. I wondered if he was worried about the old cowboy.

Then I saw what he was looking at. Ticks crawled up my legs.

They were fat and slow and probably the biggest ticks I'd ever seen in my life.

Lim swiped them off me one by one.

When we entered the farmhouse, I sat in one of the kitchen chairs and let him check my hair. He picked out a few more ticks and flung them in the sink. We did not bother to kill them. They'd have to die a slow death, sniffing the farmhouse air for blood.

Once I was done taking care of Lim in turn, I headed toward the bathroom. "I'm going to take a shower," I said.

"I wouldn't go in there, Suzy," Lim warned.

I looked at Lim and then looked back at the bathroom. Light rimmed the door and, underneath, I saw a dark puddle edge out. It was already drying onto the wood floor.

"We probably should get out of here. We're in a lot of trouble, I think," Lim said.

I grabbed the last of the bread and some canned food they had socked away. Lim looked around the house for anything we might be able to sell but it was slim pickings.

We'd killed for nothing—not even for pleasure. I wondered about the canned potatoes in my hand and couldn't decide whether a meal in my stomach was worth it all in the end.

9

WE LEFT THE farm and its dead in the heart of night and drove until daybreak. Those cows would be dead soon, too. We drove through the forgotten parts of the country. I imagined there were lots of folks like us drifting through that no-man's-land of churches and corn.

Lim told me the old man had tried to shoot him.

"Why do you think he wanted to do that? We don't have anything."

Lim didn't look away from the road. "We have a car."

"A stolen one," I said.

"He didn't know that."

I decided not to tell Lim about the man buried in the cow pen. I'd promised Lena, after all, and I figured it was bad luck to break a promise to a dead woman. A dead mother, at that.

"Are we killers?" I asked.

Lim shrugged.

We pulled into a small, bright town. One of those main street towns with the little bank next to the little church next to the little meeting house where the old women play bingo for the firefighters.

Lim decided we should eat and I couldn't argue. I hadn't had a real meal since we'd left Morris Grove.

The diner was a hideous mix of aqua and silver. Lim and I sat in a booth across from the pie display case.

The waitress was a leathery type with bad teeth. The water glasses smelled like wet dog. Lim ordered a cheeseburger and fries. I tried to order a slice of apple pie, but Lim said it wouldn't fill me up, so I got banana pancakes instead.

"Here's what I don't get," I started, thinking back to my question in the car.

Lim fidgeted with the paper placemat in front of him. His face was calm, but he couldn't stop moving. His eyes roved around the diner like he was waiting for someone.

"How come it's always what you do that defines you?" I asked.

Lim's eyes rolled back over to mine.

"I mean, I don't get it. This is a Christian country, right? But any time anyone gets to doing anything, it's just what they do that people care about."

"What are you going on about?" Lim asked. He drained half of his water, which seemed to replenish that thin sheen on his skin.

"Take Robert Hatchfield," I began.

"Robert who?"

"Robert Hatchfield. He killed young men and hid them in the basement."

"This in one of your murder magazines?"

The waitress came with the food. My banana pancakes had a small mountain of whipped cream on top, which was fast melting into a white puddle of goop. The waitress plopped a sticky carafe of syrup in front of me and dropped a few packets of butter.

"Anything else?" she croaked. She left before we could answer.

Lim shoved his burger into his mouth. Grease dripped down his chin and onto his plate.

"Yeah. I read about him a few times. I guess, I mean, why is he just a killer now? Isn't he human like the rest of us?"

"How many people'd he kill?"

"I can't remember. Over twenty, I think."

"That's a lot of people," Lim said. With that, he shoved the last bite of the burger in his mouth. My pancakes were still untouched.

"I know it's a lot of people. I'm just saying, don't you think he did other things in his life?" I started cutting my pancakes into small pieces. "Doesn't anything else count for anything? Or are we all brothers and sisters in Christ only up until the point we kill . . ."

Lim gave me a sharp glare. "Can you shut up already? Eat your food before I eat it."

I took a few bites of the pancakes. They weren't bad, but they sure weren't great.

"They killed him, you know," I said. "Lethal injection. You know what that is, right?"

Lim played with the car keys. His eyes moved from the door, to the parking lot, to his own large hands. "Guess he had it coming," was all he could say.

I poured so much syrup on my pancakes they turned dark brown and started to dissolve. I shoveled sugary bite after sugary bite into my mouth. They reminded me of the frozen kind I used to eat when I was a kid. It was one of the first things I learned how to cook, if you can call putting frozen waffles in a toaster cooking.

Outside, the cars moseyed on down the street. A woman pushed a stroller. She was young and anxious. Every few steps, she stopped to see if the baby was alright.

Every once in a while, I'd wonder what Mama had been like when Lim and I were babies. It scared me. I saw babies from time to time and they were so weak. I didn't like to think of myself so vulnerable in her arms.

The same question haunted my thoughts. What did she do to me? What did she do to Lim? Things we'll never know.

I thought of Lena's belly and the soft little curve of it. The only soft thing about her. And we'd killed it.

The waitress came by and dropped the check, a see-through receipt charging us twelve dollars for our food. She put it smack dab in the middle of a water ring and forced a smile at us. It felt like a measured assault.

"Y'all going to the pretzel parade?"

Lim and I stared at her for a moment, not knowing how to respond. I finally smiled back and asked what the pretzel parade was.

"Oh y'alls not here for the pretzel parade? Y'all gonna miss out.

They serve my favorite kind of pretzel there."

"What kind is that?" I asked.

"You gonna go?" she asked.

"Probably not," I said.

"Well what's the sense in me tellin' you my favorite if y'all not even gonna go?"

I shrugged. That was a fair question.

As Lim reached for the check, the waitress seemed to remember she was supposed to be nice to us. She smiled and leaned down toward the table, her weathered cleavage over-exposed. She licked her lips as if she salivated at the mere thought and confided, "My favorite is the gravy pretzel from Mo Ja Mo's. That gravy—" she smacked her lips "—is heaven on earth."

Her eyes turned cold as she surveyed Lim counting quarters and, on her heel, she remarked, "Not that you'll ever know."

I watched her click-clack her beaten chunky pumps off to the kitchen. I wondered if, after work, she'd steal away to try to go grab a gravy pretzel. I wondered if she even liked pretzels or if that was just some cockamamie recommendation she came up with for the tourists this time of year.

"I hate gravy," I said.

Lim finished counting the money and toppled a mishmash pile of dollars and coins onto the wet table.

As we got up to leave, I noticed an old man at a nearby table in gray suspenders holding up pants stretched thinly over his bulbous belly. I could have sworn I saw him peek at us as he shoveled loaded grits into his mouth.

And the woman and her three children. Why was she looking at us? She fidgeted with the pearl buttons on her pretty pink cardigan. She smoothed her chestnut hair with manicured hands as she looked at us in assault rifle pitter-patters.

I put my hands on Lim's back and physically urged him to move faster.

I didn't need to look at the television news broadcast playing above the pie case. I already knew whose photos they were showing.

10

TIME SLOWED AS we drove out of town.

I started to see my life as a finite series of moments and I tried to catch each one as it passed. It was like trying to catch fireflies. Every time I thought I snagged one, I opened my hand to look at the pretty light and it disappeared.

"Do you think we can go to the movies tonight?" I asked Lim.

He didn't answer, so I figured that was a no. He'd hardly said a word since we'd left the diner.

I had a weird recollection looking at his face. I thought of a time when Mama'd railed so hard against me and I'd gone crying into the bathroom.

Just remembering it set my skin on fire.

I rolled down the window for some air. I tried to catch the

present moment but all I thought about was the past.

In the bathroom, I'd removed a flat blade from a cheap razor. I'd started to run it along my arm's delicate flesh. I had wanted to bleed out and sleep forever. I had wanted to cut her hands out from inside of me. I had wanted to stop feeling her fingers—her fingers which reached everywhere.

But Lim had stayed my hand. I'd looked at him then like I looked at him now.

He was so big, but so small. One man alone in the world, born to a mother with a wolf's heart hiding in a sheep's skin. It was just the two of us. I didn't know if Lim loved me. But I knew I didn't want to leave him and that somehow being by his side felt safer than the unknown black void of death.

I thought of Lena and her baby swirling in a dark vortex in the sky. I thought of Lena's hands as I'd hit her head with the shovel.

Even as I had swung down hard at her head, again and again, her hands had stayed low over her belly. She hadn't tried to protect herself. Even in those last moments of brain power, she had thought of the baby inside her.

And I thought of my own mother and I felt acute terror.

"Lim." I suddenly tugged on the sleeve of his arm.

"What?" he asked.

"Is there an afterlife? Do you think there is one?"

"How the hell am I supposed to know?"

"I don't want to see her again."

The silence between us felt like a caress. It was intimate.

I closed my eyes and all I saw was me floating in the blackness. I was naked and without hands to shield my body. I was just breasts and a crotch, a mouth and a belly. A defenseless body floating in the lonely dark.

When I awoke, it was nighttime again.

Lim was outside the car pumping gas.

I stared through the windshield at a young woman at the pump in front of us. Her posture held the normal bracing tension of a woman alone at night. She kept her eyes mostly locked on the gas meter but occasionally would glance over at our car, and at Lim.

She was a pretty girl with blonde hair down to mid-back. It was shiny and straight. She wore a wide headband, a polo shirt, and one of those chunky pearl necklaces with the satin ribbon ties.

She saw me staring at her and looked away quickly. When she looked again and saw me still staring, she hurried to put the gas pump back.

I signaled to Lim and he got back in the car.

"We should follow her," I said.

She started to roll off. Lim started the engine and we followed casually at a few lengths behind. I wondered if she was wondering about us right now. I wondered if fear had started to crawl up her spine and shake the breath out of her.

The girl drove down the lonesome two-lane highway through never-ending corn fields. The only lights were her headlights and ours.

"Flash her," I said.

Lim flashed his headlights at her three times. She slowed for a moment before speeding up again. She was indecisive.

"Do it again," I said.

He pulled up close on her tail and flashed the high beams a few more times. In each burst of light I could see a swarm of insects milling about in the night air. The darkness was alive.

After the third flash, the girl pulled off the road and slowed to a stop. I exchanged a quick and knowing glance with Lim. We needed her car. Lim pulled up beside where she had stopped and I rolled down my window.

The girl rolled her window down a few inches in response. I couldn't make out her face in the dark. A few gnats flew in and flirted with my lips. They tickled my eyelids.

"You left your gas cap open," I said.

"Oh, really?" Her voice sounded so unsure of itself, as if she were surprised to hear sound come out of her own mouth.

"Yeah. We saw it as we were driving. That's why we were flashing you. Here, we'll back up and let you take a look."

"Oh, thank you. You don't have to wait," she assured us.

She'd feel too guilty not to get out and look. Every girl in the world was taught not to trust her gut. Every girl in the world knew she was the fool in the play.

"It's no bother," I said.

I rolled up the window and Lim backed up a bit on the road.

"When she gets out, hit her," I told him.

The girl got out of the car when she saw we were a sufficient length away. She hurried over to the gas cap. When she saw it was closed, she looked up at us with a look of cartoonish terror across her face. In the hazy glow of our headlamps, she looked like a ghost in a low budget movie.

But then I saw her fear and I was familiar enough to know the dead didn't fear.

Lim floored the gas. It was so quick I didn't catch her expression before we hit her. I'd never seen a person hit by a car before. I had expected the girl to bounce up onto the top of the car and to roll off dramatically like they showed in the movies.

That didn't happen.

She fell down and actually went under the carriage. When Lim backed up, we rolled over some part of her body like a speedbump. Our headlamps illuminated what was left: she was barely moving.

"Let's move her," I said. Lim and I got out of the car and walked over to the girl. Her face wasn't pretty anymore. It shocked me how little blood there was. She reminded me of a lump of putty now; she was bulging and dented in all the wrong places. Human form was so fragile.

Lim picked her up with ease. As he lifted the girl, she spat out blood in a slow, drool-like fashion and soon her insides were spilling down her pretty pink polo. If she lived, this would be quite a story for her, I thought. This would be the night she would tell all her future boyfriends about before they slept together for the first time and those boys, not really giving a shit, would hold her close and tell her they'd protect her. And the girl—a girl like that—she'd be too dumb to know love was just a means to an end.

We dumped her body in the cornfield. Lim asked if we should kill her but I said no. I don't know why I said no. She looked pretty young to me. She reminded me of Alice. Alice used to tell me how her parents were looking for her. She just knew it. That was something I could only imagine. Mama wouldn't have cared.

The girl started to make a strange noise. She was trying to cry but probably some part of her was too mangled to do it right. I crouched down next to her body and placed my hand on her battered face. She wailed as if my touch burned.

It was an odd sensation to watch a girl who was near to dying spend the little energy she had trying to scoot away from me. I wondered if my presence were worse than death. I didn't know why she was trying to get away from us. We'd already said we weren't going to kill her, after all.

11

HER CAR WAS much sleeker than Mama's. The insides were leather and felt cool to the touch.

Lim didn't waste time in getting out of there. I rolled down the window and the hot air licked my face as we rocketed along that pocket of nowhere.

There were stars in the sky. I looked up at them and wondered if that girl was staring at them right now.

"Do you think she'll die?" I asked.

I knew Lim didn't really want to think about that, one way or the other. But I was curious. I wanted to know if that place in the thick of the corn would be her last stop. I thought about her mom.

I was always thinking of moms. And then I thought of Lena and her baby, warm in the womb. I wondered, looking at the stars, how long it might take for a womb to get cold once the mother died. I wondered if blood kept pumping even after the mother stopped thinking. I figured bodies tried their damnedest to bring life into the world.

And there we were, I thought, the knights of death. The white markers on the road zipped by like bullets and we dodged all of them. Zip. Zip. Zip. If we were standing still, those things might've looked pretty long. But we weren't standing still; we were on the road with places to be. Those little markers didn't mean squat.

"Lim," I said.

"Jesus, I don't know if she's dead. Maybe. Good chance of it." His eyes looked small and cold in the soft glow of the car controls.

"What's going to happen to us?" I asked.

"If you ask another question right now, I'm gonna put you in the cornfield, too," he said, his voice low and even. I laughed loudly at that and stuck my head out the window like a dog. I let my hair really whip around in the wind and caught some bugs' final moments across my face.

Refreshed, I ducked back inside and grabbed the girl's purse from the floor of the passenger's seat.

I found her school identification. Her name was Amber Pugliatti. She also had some gift cards, a gas station credit card, and about thirty dollars, cash.

"Not much we can use here," I said.

Lim shrugged his big shoulders. There was something wrong with that big head of his, atop his giant, hulking body. Something out of this world that was plunked into it, happenstance-like, right before

I was.

He didn't seem to have any grasp on the future. The future was some fairy-tale to him. All Lim thought about was the right-now, the here-now, the this-moment-we're-living.

I was vaguely aware there were people out there paying lots of money to think like Lim did. Behind his too-small eyes, all he focused on was the present. The need for survival was so strong in his gaze and manner I couldn't help but to feel protected by him.

For everyone else, Lim was the scariest person they'd ever met.

12

THERE WAS ENOUGH cash between us to get a room for the night. We pulled into a place that rented by the hour and advertised cable. The cashier was in the parking lot in a narrow glass box. We slipped her the cash through a slot in the glass.

While we were waiting for the room key, a short prostitute who called herself Milly sidled up next to Lim. She looked loopy and hungry with stick-thin legs perched atop platform heels.

Lim wrapped an arm around the junkie and let her hang on him. Her hand, one of the nails torn off, rubbed his chest while she slurred something or other. I could only make out the word, "fun."

I took the room key from under the slot. The cashier refused to make eye contact with me, which was for the better. I thought it must have been nice to have that kind of tunnel vision. All around the glass cube was mayhem but the cashier was safe in an oasis of calm.

I felt like that sometimes, too. They were times I didn't want to think about.

Lim and I walked to room five with Milly lurking behind us.

When we reached the door, a topless woman darted out from the adjacent room. Mascara ran down from her bloodshot eyes across her tear-soaked face. The door to the room slammed behind her and she started to beat it with her fists, her breasts bouncing with every thwack.

For the first time since we'd left Mama, it felt like home.

Milly asked the crying girl, Jamie, if she was okay. The funny thing was that Jamie didn't seem to care her breasts were out—hanging, flopping and bouncing. I felt like a cat watching a toy on a string. No matter what circus surrounded us, it was hard not to stare at Jamie's breasts.

I looked at Lim; he wasn't looking at her body. He was looking at her eyes. Through her eyes. My brother did that sometimes. I'd watch him stare at people and get the sense he was seeing more than I could. I looked and saw bodies flinging this way and that. He looked and saw the soul-map inside.

Jamie had started jabbering about some guy who I guess decided not to pay her, after all. And then her eyes found Lim's and her jabbering slowed to a soft hum I didn't think she was aware she was making.

We all went into the room. I was somewhat aware of my laughing and smiling. I knew there were small questions slipping out of my throat—the same stock ones everyone exhaled in first meetings.

"I like your hair," Jamie said and she started running her fingers through it.

"Do you want something to cover up with?" I asked.

Jamie shrugged, asked Lim for a cigarette, and flopped on the bed with one of her elbows propping her head up. Straight red hair poured over her shoulder. The box-dyed red, bright like pizza sauce, contrasted prettily with her skin's milkiness. She idly stroked her bare stomach with one of her darkly freckled arms. Her index finger went in and out of her belly button as it traversed that soft plane of flesh. She wasn't subtle.

Lim handed her a cigarette. She put it in her mouth and stared at him. There was an invitation in her eyes, but Lim didn't seem interested.

He bent down to light it for her. Jamie held the cigarette steady in her lips and inhaled for a long time. The smoke came out of her nose. Her back arched; it looked pleasurable. They said smoking made you old but she looked ten years younger getting that first bit of nicotine. Her body braced and relaxed like a kitten stretching out in a new bed.

Jamie had a worn look about her, but I still found her beautiful.

Milly was much less relaxed. She fidgeted and paced around the room. There was a chipped coffee pot she went to several times. Each time, she'd pick it up and look inside as if she expected to find something new.

"Why you got that crackhead in here?" Jamie asked, the cigarette dwindling fast between her fingers.

Lim looked over at Milly. No matter who people were talking to and no matter what people were doing—if they were in the same room as Lim—then somewhere in the back of their minds, they were aware of his presence.

When people were around a man like Lim, it was like they could smell blood in the water and prayed it wasn't theirs. The stiffness they felt—the tingle on their neck—that was by design. That was biology telling them, *There is the potential here for violence.*

"Get out," Lim said to Milly.

She had her head halfway in the damn coffee pot again when Lim grabbed her by the arm. She shrieked and swatted at him as he dragged her across the room. Jamie laughed.

I took a hard look at Jamie while Lim flung the other prostitute outside.

I had a strange desire to see all of her. I wanted to see her vocal cords and how they danced as she spoke. I wanted to see how blackened her lungs were. I wanted to reach up between her legs and shake her innards around. She was beautiful.

"You're looking at me awful serious," she said.

Behind me, Lim closed the door. The metal scraped as he slid the lock closed.

"Close those blinds," Lim said to me.

Jamie wasn't dumb. A shadow crossed her eyes for a split second and she saw the monster in me. She had the look of a person who had done bad things and who knew a trick or two when she saw it.

I went to the blinds and turned my head to watch. Jamie perched on her knees on the bed. Between her and the door was Lim. His shadow dwarfed the topless redhead and made her skin look a shade of yellow, like early decay. I wondered what colors Lim was going to paint with that woman.

I took the window rod in my hand and suddenly realized the full power I had in those briefest of seconds. If I delayed closing the blinds, maybe Lim would turn his head. Maybe she would have a moment to run out the door. When people prayed to God, I wondered, were they praying to Him or were they praying to me? I couldn't quite see a difference in that moment.

I rotated the rod a few times and then we were alone.

"Don't hurt me," Jamie said. Her voice was softer, but she didn't seem scared. It was the voice of someone trying to negotiate.

"I'll suck your cock. You can fuck me in the ass. You can piss on me," Jamie offered. She was scooting away from him ever so slightly. I could see more of her out of his shadow than was in. She was clever.

"Just don't hurt me, okay?" Jamie said. She kept talking as she edged away from him.

"I have a kid," she added. For the first time, I saw her breasts heave. Her heart was pumping adrenaline. It only took one surge—a big heave of the breast—and she was up from the bed, darting toward the door.

She got to the door in a panic. She kept twisting the knob but it wouldn't budge.

By the time she realized it was locked, Lim was behind her.

He grabbed her by the hair and punched her in the face. Her nose busted a bloody stream running down into her mouth. She gasped and groaned but didn't scream.

"She's being pretty good, Lim," I said.

Lim threw her back on the bed.

"I'll do anything," she said as she drank and licked the blood pouring from her nose.

I watched her, the way her muscles twitched. She was trying to survive. It stirred a feeling inside of me. It felt like love, but it wasn't. Just a shiny fake penny glinting through the dirt.

I felt like I was looking at a mirror, watching Jamie try to survive, and I liked what I saw for the first time.

"Give me your money," I told Jamie.

Jamie looked at me. It was the look of a woman asking another woman, "How can you do this to me?"

As if we were all connected in an invisible network of vaginas. As if I owed her something.

"Give me your money and you can go," I repeated.

Lim settled his pinpoints on me and I didn't much care. He could kill me if he liked. I was going to fight him for it, though. I'd fought all my life and I stood there in that motel room, thinking to myself, *What was I fighting to hold onto?* My breasts? Didn't want them. There was a fire in my gut, and it was a roaring fire saying to all who dared to slight me, "You've seen wrong. I am not the girl I pretend to be. I am a beast."

My eyes dropped to Jamie's breasts and for the first time since I'd met her, she wrapped an arm around herself. Her other hand reached into her pocket and pulled out lots of small bills. She handed them over to me. I felt the money in my hand—the damp, grainy papers. There was something empowering about feeling lots of cash in your hands.

"All of it," I said.

Jamie reached deeper and extracted a few last bills. She tucked her hand into her pants and pulled out a few more from who-knows-where. She tossed the last bill at me, a small act of defiance.

Lim took a step closer. I thought he might kill us both. But he didn't. He stared at me, waiting.

"Now go," I told her.

Jamie didn't look at Lim as she scurried past. She slid the lock this time and left quickly.

Lim sat on the bed with his back to me.

"Are you mad?" I asked.

He didn't respond.

I sat on the ground and began counting the bills. There were lots of them, but they were mostly small change.

For the duration of my counting, I was aware of Lim's breathing. It was heavy and slow. He was like a machine I couldn't turn off. I wondered if anyone would be able to turn him off.

"Lim?" I asked.

No response.

"Lim, do you remember Dad?"

"How much money do we have?"

"A hundred thirty. Not bad, really. But—"

"I remember he didn't want a girl," Lim said. He turned to me. "You were born and he said you were nothing but a cunt."

I could still smell Jamie. She had left behind an odor of sex and blood, or maybe we were smelling the memories of others who had wallowed in room five before us.

"He said that when I was a baby?"

"He called you a cunt. He was standing over you with these little sewing scissors. He turned to me and he said, 'I'm going to cut her open and fuck her.' I told him not to because . . ." Lim paused and turned away again.

He stood up and paced the room. His shoulders rolled as he walked. My brother was a lion in a cage.

"Well, doesn't matter why I said it. He told me there was nothing I could do about it. He had a smile on his face when he said it, had his hand already on you. I was sure he was going to do it."

Lim settled into a calm. And then he said, "So I cut him. With something bigger than sewing scissors."

"But Mama said he left with a whore and never came back."

"Mama did say that."

Lim shook out his last cigarette, lit it, and looked at me again. I saw a boy but I knew it was just me wanting to see it. It was hard to think of Lim as a boy, big as he was. He never really was a child, after all. And I never was, neither.

"But what did you do with him?"

Lim smoked half his cigarette in one drag.

"Who cares what happens to the meat after it's off the bone?"

I turned back to the bills and piled them into a neat stack. I had no memory of my father. All my life I'd only known Mama. The thought of her and her hands made me tremble. I wanted to cry but there was nothing to cry about.

There was something sadder that took over me in that motel room. Sadder than sadness as I knew it. I think I wanted to die.

And then I thought of my body, of all the soft and feminine parts. And I wanted to cut myself open, too. I wanted to cut myself and leave those parts to rot in the sink. I'd let Lim decide what to do with them. He was a master at hiding parts of bodies, it seemed, and he could hide me, too. Better to dissect myself than to have to jiggle around this world like a cheap plaything. Better to be dead than to be like Jamie, sucking and fucking for fives and tens in the heart of night, and for what? I wanted to tear my breast off in that moment and force feed it to the world. I wanted to maim.

"Are you telling the truth about Dad?" I asked. It was foolish to ask. I wanted him to take pity on me. I wanted him to pretend it was a lie.

"No reason to lie now," Lim said, and he got in bed, lay on his back, and shut his eyes. It was simple as that for Lim.

And I didn't dare cry about it.

13

THERE WAS SOMETHING about being on the road for so long that made me itch for a place to put my head. Home was the rising stench of laundry and the little hairs I saw in the sink while I brushed my teeth. Little hairs I did nothing about.

The road's unfamiliar filth offered no comfort. The road was a constant reminder that everything, including me, could disappear from the earth with a little time and a little distance. Nothing was so big it couldn't be passed by and that was what the road spoke to all who traveled it. She whispered in our ears, "Someone was here before you and someone will be here after."

There was no lover as cold as she.

Lim applied pressure to the pulse in my wrist. The touch of his meaty fingers made my heart jump.

"Stop your nerves," he said.

There was a county fair in the near distance. For the last several miles, we had seen billboards and signs advertising it. Hand-painted pictures of ferris wheels and smiling children. One unsightly billboard showed a woman with mouth ajar, a bright red hot dog ready to be consumed. She had seemed to wink at us, as if to say, "Stop by and I'll eat you, too."

I asked Lim if we could go.

"What, you want to ride the ferris wheel? That's kids' stuff," he said.

I looked at my hands. I traced the thin, intersecting lines with my eyes. Did they show something about me I didn't know? I wondered where I could find my childhood in the palm of my hand. Was it predestined to be so short? The children on the billboards who were smiling and eating funnel cakes—would their palms show different lines than mine?

"I want to see the pigs."

"God, you can see a pig any damn time. I'm not stopping for a pig."

"I want to see the show pigs."

"What in the hell is a show pig?"

"Please. We don't need to stay long. I just want to see them, is all."

I'd dreamt about Alice in the motel last night while I'd lain on the floor after Jamie left. She wasn't burnt up in my dream. She and I ran through the woods together, hand in hand. I imagined her sitting in the backseat. If she were there with us, she would have added to the clamor. I could almost hear her young voice through the vent . . .

"Please, let's stop to see the pigs. Please!"

And the clatter of chain that followed. The chains always followed.

Lim pulled into a yellow-tape parking lot. The cordoned perimeter reminded me of scenes from my favorite copy of *True Crime*.

Psychics were sometimes interviewed or quoted in the magazine. They always talked about getting a bad feeling about *this* or getting a bad feeling about *that*. Well, I had a bad feeling as we pulled into that parking lot. There was the faintest scent of burning. Was it rubber?

Or Alice?

I remembered the smoke filling the living room. Her face peered out at us from the basement, so faint an outline it could have been a ghost. Alice and I had dreamed of being free together. Our dream was a billboard's fantasy. We wanted to ride the ferris wheel and laugh.

And then I thought of the newspapers and TVs. And how my face in black-and-white would look like the rest of them. How I was the monster I pretended not to be.

Alice died an angel. She was not me.

The world never accepted the unwanted child. Firmer than any scripture was the belief that no matter how ugly or horrid a child could be, at least the child's mother would love it. Perhaps the worst damage to society had been the perpetuation of this myth . . . for it orphaned Lim and me. It orphaned all of us. The unwanted. The abused. The raped.

The Unloved.

We stood in line for tickets. All around us ran children and families. Fathers shouted after sons and mothers twirled their daughters' hair. In their midst were at least two murderers, though they were none the wiser.

Fried food filled the air. Beyond the entrance, bright lights and music came in waves as the rides and games cycled through their various visitors. By the time Lim forked over the five dollars for admission, I was lost in thought and near trembling.

There was a girl in a butterfly-printed shirt, all but six years old. Her dad stuck his tongue out at her and it made her laugh so hard she snorted. Her hair was as dark and frizzy as my mother's hair. I wondered if my mom were like her once. I wondered how the world made its villains and why it never apologized for making them.

"Don't hurt her," I said under my breath.

I pushed away from Lim and went farther into the crowds. I looked back and saw his hulking figure slowly making his way behind me.

"Suzy!" he called.

I didn't want to wait for Lim. I wanted a moment to myself. I wanted to see if the dream Alice and I had could have ever been real. I rushed forward and away from Lim. I wound my way through the thickening crowd like a spy on a mission.

The animal tent was a garish, striped thing. It looked like I'd imagined a circus tent would. While colorful and bright from a distance, it was obvious the tent had seen better days when I got up close. Mud and yellowed splotches decorated the thing from floor to top.

Patrons milled around, disinterested in anything but gorging on more funnel cake and cotton candy. One woman almost deep-throated a hot dog while her infant incessantly screamed in her arms with tiny hands clawing blindly for a breast. The uncontrollable human noise of the crowd stressed me.

I ducked under the flap and was met with intense and stale heat. The inside of the tent was packed from wall to wall with laughing and gawking bystanders. Two teenage boys in sports jerseys blocked my view.

The smell and crowd filled me with dread. It wasn't what I was imagining as a home for intelligent show pigs. I had pictured an idyllic pasture or private pen where children could kneel and pet them. I'd imagined adequate space and fresh air, at the very least. Someplace green. There was nothing green here. It was all various shades of yellow and brown, like a painting of rot.

I pushed past the two boys and saw what everyone was laughing at.

There were three small pens each half full of pig shit. One pig had three legs and tottered around fruitlessly. He fell each time he tried to stand as he slipped over and over in his own defecation. The other pig was without half a snout. His oinks sounded freakish and pained.

"Listen to that fucking thing," the boy said behind me.

The boy's friend leaned in close to my ear, "Probably how you sound in bed, huh?"

I turned around and stared at the two milky-skinned teenagers. There must've been something about the way I looked at them that stilled their cocks. They took a step back from me, eyeballing each other as if I were the freak.

"Let's get out of here," the teenager said. His friend oinked at me and grabbed his dick.

I turned back to the pigs.

The third was the saddest of all—a paraplegic. It lay in its own waste and stared out at the crowd with roving, frightened eyes. The sign above the three pens read, "Animal Freak Show," in bold, blocky letters.

A little boy with hair gelled into vertical spikes poked at the paraplegic pig while his father chatted baseball with the man next to him.

"Dad, look," the boy said, and he poked the legless pig again. "When I poke him, his eye moves."

He poked him again.

The half-snouted pig nearby made louder and louder noises. It was yelling. It was pleading.

Or it was dying.

And they all found it so funny.

"I'm gonna touch his eye," the boy said. "Dad, what do you think he'll do if I touch his eye? Do you think he'll roll over?"

The dad didn't look at the boy. The boy went ahead with his experiment, his outreached hand nearing the pig's eye.

I was not an especially violent person. Really, I was terribly shy in a crowd, but I guess I'd done something terrible to that boy. Something violent and not quite right. By the time the father lifted me off the boy, the child struggled to breathe. Now he made funny sounds like a balloon losing all its air. And something black was around his eye—the imprint of my fist.

The boy's father—hands firm on my shoulders—stared at me as though he wanted to kill me, if only he had it in him.

"You little bitch," he said.

The other man yelled for security like a scared child. "Security!" he screeched, "Securiteeee!"

And then came Lim like an angel through the crowd. He had a metal hoe in his hand.

"Jesus, Bill, watch ou—!"

I swore I saw a tooth fly out of the man's head as he went down. He took me down with him in the midst of his fall.

I hit the ground hard and my lungs filled with the smell of pig shit.

The subsequent silence gave me hope. It was but for a moment that I was sure all the world's laughter stopped. Lim had a way about him, he did.

I was now on the legless pig's level and our eyes locked. I saw that pig's missing legs and I knew, without asking, it wasn't born that way. Someone had made it that way.

There was no evil in the world that was not man's work.

And there was no man in the world that was not woman's work.

We were locked in each other's embrace, fucking each other till we all fell apart at the joints. I wanted no part of it. I wanted to kill the pigs, if only so no one would ever laugh at them again.

I wanted to take a hoe to the whole of humanity like Lim did to that man. Knock the teeth out of the fucking human race. A pain rang through my head from ear to ear. I must've knocked something real good during the fall.

"This isn't Moses," Lim had said.

But weren't we all Moses? I wished, with my lungs full of manure and my head ringing, that someone would put me out of my misery.

I thought of the blackness of sleep and wondered, could death be any different? There was something pleasant about the thought of an endless sleep.

I turned my head and I saw Lim staring down at me.

"This isn't Moses," I said, or at least I thought I said it, and he raised the metal hoe over his head.

He'd never hurt me. He wouldn't. No. Not really, anyhow.

The last thing I saw was the dead of his eyes. There was a pain so deep it faded to bliss.

And as the sirens sounded, I drifted into the sleep of the dreamless.

14

"**LIFE WITHOUT DREAMS** is hardly any life at all," Hank Riley told me as he unpacked a loaf of cheap white bread from his backpack.

He put a piece of bread in my hand and I took a bite out of it, which caused him to stare at me hard. It reminded me of the way the teachers back at Morris Grove used to look at me. It was a familiar look of high inquisition—an effort to decide if I was doing something bad on purpose or if I was a didn't-know-better kind of girl.

"It's for them," Hank Riley said, and he gestured out to the desperate ducks who were flipping and flapping on the bank of the pond.

It really was a picturesque scene, that pond. Hank Riley and his wife, Carol, had taken me there the night Lim was sentenced to life in prison. I had been like a stone that day, waiting to be chucked and forgotten.

I hadn't been allowed to attend the trial. A stipulation of my placement with the Rileys was that I couldn't see or have contact with Lim. I had to wait to hear the verdict second-hand. It had been all over the news. Lots of women in pretty hair-dos had smiled as they thrust out their chests and exclaimed to the public that my brother was going to die in a cage. They had held their microphones with tenderly salacious grips as if the thought of it had made them wet.

Hank Riley led me down to the same bench we had all sat on the night I knew my brother would forever be in prison. I worried about Lim sometimes. I knew he could defend himself but I worried about his heart. If I were more honest, I worried about my place in his heart. I missed having my older brother by my side.

Sometimes I slipped out of my room at night at Hank Riley's. I walked the streets in my nightgown. I tempted fate. I tempted murder.

There was a rage so deep inside of me that wanted a man to dare try to kill me. There was a hate so deep inside of me that wanted me to dare just die. When I returned at night from my secret walks, I cried in such a way that no one could hear me.

I cried because Lim was the only person who might've ever loved me, at least enough to see to it that any hand that harmed me lost the ability to harm at all. What did it say about me that my one true guardian angel was the earth's devil?

"You still have the scar from where he hit you and yet you still love him," Hank Riley remarked. He was always pointing at something with his words. He was a good-looking guy. He took care of himself, as people were fond of saying. He worked out and had a clean shave. He wore a style that spoke of wealth. His hands weren't soft but they weren't calloused either.

"This scar is nothing," I said.

Hank Riley continued to stare. I could see in his warm brown eyes that he didn't believe me. He seemed to have an endless well of pity for me, though I couldn't have understood why. Sometimes it made me feel alright and other times it filled me with anger. What right did he have, I thought, to take pity on anyone? Pity was worthless.

"I know you said you don't want to talk about when he kidnapped you, Suzy, but I want you to know, that as long as you keep that to yourself, you'll never heal. Not fully, anyhow."

Hank Riley leaned down on his knees and looked up at me. I looked at his hands and I tried to remember Lim's hands.

Lim's hands that could dwarf melons.

"Do you like me?" I asked.

He laughed; the question caught him off guard. "Like you? You've been living with us for two years now. Carol and I adore you."

"You wouldn't think as much of me if you actually knew me," I said.

"That's not true," he said. There was a certainty to his statement that made me feel it must not be true.

"You don't want to know what happened on the trip," I repeated. I felt like I was saying the same things over and over for the past two years.

When Carol and Hank Riley had taken me in, they'd kept a

measured distance at first. I'd overheard the counselor advising them to be consistent, stable, and firm yet warm. Everything had been about sustenance and bedding. Things like clean towels and a cooked breakfast were paramount to my healing, the counselor had said.

And yet, as I looked at those noisy, fat ducks, part of me wanted to smash their quacking heads in. There was no amount of sausage and eggs, no small comfort of middle-class living, that could take away that urge, or so it felt to me. Some itching didn't have a cure.

My rage didn't stop for the pain of others. It was a coldness I must have hidden well from Hank Riley, for in the two years I had lived with him, I had managed to convince him I was worth keeping around.

"I do want to know. I very much want to know what happened. I want you to be able to trust me." He paused for a moment. "Is it Carol you're worried about? I know, before, you said you don't feel like she wants you around sometimes."

I shrugged, "I don't really worry. It's just what I know—that if you heard the truth—you wouldn't like me much. I hear what you and everyone else says about Lim. I know you don't like him. So why would you like me?"

"Your brother kidnapped and assaulted you—"

"He never assaulted me."

"He smashed your head in and permanently scarred you with a backhoe at a county fair after kidnapping you and taking you on a murder rampage. You could have died." Hank Riley reached out his hand and his fingers touched my forearm.

I shrugged off his touch and grabbed a piece of bread. I balled it up in my hand and threw it at a duck. It hit the duck on the side and bounced off. The stupid bird wasted its opportunity staring at me while a pigeon flew in and looted the bread ball in its much tinier beak.

"Don't do that," Hank Riley said. His voice sounded a little more tired than usual.

"Why not? It's not like the duck's gonna fight me," I said.

"You know you shouldn't do that. It's not nice. Come on," he said. I realized then as I noted his begging eyes that he desperately needed to believe I was a victim.

It was his wife, Carol, who would whisper worrisome things to him in the middle of the night. Bad things about me. True things. She would tell him she thought I was troubled. Hank Riley would tell her she was wrong and that all I needed was their loving support. I'd peer at them through the crack in the bedroom door. There was a coldness between them in bed whenever they spoke of me.

Hank Riley needed me. Maybe for Lim, I would've lied. Maybe even for Alice, whose burnt remains they never found but, then again, I wasn't sure anyone even looked.

I couldn't tell him the truth, though. I couldn't explain to him that Carol had the heebies about me because she was right. Part of her sensed me watching them from the darkness. Part of her knew I was thinking maybe, just maybe, there would be a moment at night when I could trespass across the veil of all that was orderly, take a knife to their bellies, and let them bleed out all over their luxurious bed sheets. Truth was, they were tiny and vulnerable in that big bed of theirs.

I said, "I'm hungry," instead, and Hank Riley got up from the bench, a little less pep to his gait.

15

MY FIRST PAYING job was at a hot dog drive-thru operation called "Jack's." It was a little white hut in a cordoned off section of parking lot. There was a small red overhang and a cheap picket sign that said, "Enter here" for the drive-thru. There was no set uniform. All I had to do was show up on time, keep the dogs hot, keep the condiment containers full, and serve people pork parts with a smile on my face.

I'll admit it took me a bit to get the smile right, but in a month's time I was a favorite of Mr. Jack, himself. He was an older man with a scraggly red beard and a hideous pock-marked face. He was one of those men whose appearance shamelessly showcased the darkness of his soul. Hank Riley didn't seem to like him that much.

Mr. Jack had a friend, Milton, who was just released from the same prison Lim was in, and he'd tell me stories sometimes in exchange for small favors.

"Hey, you show me your titties and I'll tell you about the time your brother broke a guard's arm in two," he said to me one afternoon.

I lifted my t-shirt and showed him my breasts. I didn't care much about them, anyway. I let him get a good look while his hand neared his crotch. Just as he started stroking, I lowered my shirt.

"Well that ain't right," he said and let out a laugh.

I turned my back to Milton and dug a spoon around in the relish container which needed frequent mixing so the contents wouldn't separate. It reminded me of snot. Whenever Milton was around, it was hard not to be hyper-aware of his presence. It felt as though at any point he might come up behind me and force himself on me. I knew he had considered it.

But there was something about me which made people hesitate. I was the black sheep, the sheep with teeth, the sheep even the wolf wouldn't eat.

There was something gratifying about people's hesitations and concerns when around me. Maybe I'd never needed Lim, after all. Though then again, there was no wolf fiercer than Mama and sometimes a mighty big wolf needed another wolf to take it down.

It was unwise to underestimate a weak opponent. Even a weak man could find someone strong to fight his battles for him. Even weak people sometimes had charming tongues and even the strong sometimes had listening ears.

A customer pulled up to the window. She was older, with short, bleached hair and small, delicate gold hoop earrings. She wore one of those staple-of-the-season v-neck sweaters, her décolletage an artificial shade of nut brown.

I handed her the chili dog she ordered and in return she shoved a wad of crumpled, sticky napkins into my hand. "Do you mind?" she sneered.

"Oh hey, Delores," Milton said from behind me. The woman's eyes filled with fear when she heard Milton's voice. She averted her gaze straight ahead and drove off in a hurry.

"You know her?" I asked.

"Kind of. Her husband owes me money," he said. I gave him a side-eye and he shrugged his hands into his pockets.

"For what?" I asked.

"What the fuck do you care?" he asked and sat back down, his eyes set straight ahead, not looking at anything in particular.

I never really believed any word that came out of Milton's mouth. In a way, Milton was a type more dangerous than Lim because Milton had an ego to sate. He was the type to kill just to prove he could and not because he needed to. I sometimes worried he would come after me one day. I worried he would wrap his hands around my throat to get a hard-on. I didn't much like Milton, but I did like the way he talked about Lim. He had respect for my brother and maybe, after all, that's what kept him in line.

Yeah, who was I fooling? Nobody kept their hands off a woman because a woman didn't want it . . . there was always some man who loomed in the distance threatening something worse. I was a fucking heifer as far as Milton was concerned—an idle, blinking bulb he sometimes squinted at funny.

"You never did say," I said.

"Say what?"

"Why Lim broke the guard's arm."

"Oh," Milton laughed, "you won't believe me if I tell you."

I shrugged, "I'd believe about anything about Lim."

"'Cause of you, he broke it. That guard was new on the job, didn't know about Lim's weird takin' to his sister." Milton chortled.

I felt my cheeks getting hot.

"Lim was rubbing him the wrong way and you gotta understand some of these guards, they like to try to take the big guys down a notch right off the bat. Helps them keep control. Well he said something about you being a nice piece of ass, and man oh man, did I never-ever hear a bone snap quite like this guy's. Lim got time in the hole and somethin' special for that one. I worry about your brother, you see," he said.

I peered over at him hard. Milton had a snakish smile on his face.

"Why's that?"

"I worry one day, on account of you, that boy's gonna get himself killed. Can't go breaking arms forever without someone breaking you. Now that's a fact." He paused and pretended to look at his nails. "So anyway, what'd you do to get him all riled up so easy like that? You suck his cock?"

I shook my head. I knew better than to let Milton get me angry.

Truth was, I didn't know why Lim defended me so. It was something different from love and it wasn't pity. If I could have put a name to it, I would have.

16

HANK RILEY AND Carol took me to see the monseigneur at the cathedral downtown. It was considered a special trip and I was made to wear a dress for it. The dress cinched my waist and made my curves too pronounced. I slouched to try to hide my figure, but there was no way to keep an idle man's eyes off me. As we walked along the city streets, the hot air thick on my face, I could feel the construction workers repairing a pothole look at me. I didn't like it.

Carol touched the crook of my arm as we passed the men, as though she were trying to draw me into her protection. It was a funny thing to imagine—Carol protecting me. She was so delicate as to be porcelain. I felt I could give her a rough shake and she might shatter all over the pavement.

We were seeing the monseigneur partly at my request. I'd stupidly written the church asking them some questions and apparently my email ended up on the desk of the monseigneur, himself, who had—I took it—earned his honor in part by being so engaged with the community at large. He asked to meet with me. I told Hank Riley, and then he told his wife, who was from a big Irish Catholic family, and there we were, traipsing through the city to see a holy man.

It was so absurd that I began laughing on the steps of the cathedral. I was chasing God and Lim was chasing death. My thighs jiggled as I walked up the stairs and I thought of Lena. I thought of her little toned body and her soft belly. I thought of Lena and all the unborn children of the world. What did God do with all those unborn children, I wondered.

At the doors of the cathedral, I stared up at the tall stone facade which was interrupted only for bright stained glass and religious tableaus. I was somewhat familiar with the iconography, seeing as we did have a Bible in the house, but faith felt so hollow to me in word.

In life, though, staring up at the towering stone building, I understood the allure of religion.

Hank Riley held the door open for us. I saw him flash Carol a hopeful glance as we walked inside. I knew they took my email to the church as a sign I was getting better. In part, I think Hank Riley interpreted it as validation of his choice to take me in, and seeing as anything of "God" made Carol happy, they were both on some weird vicarious high leading me through the cathedral doors.

The inside of the cathedral was hot and sticky. We walked through a hallway past tables of flyers, pamphlets, and prayer cards, until we arrived at an office where a chubby woman in a hideous floral smock greeted us.

"And you must be Suzy," she said, taking my hand in her own wrinkled ones. She smelled of rot. Her smile was warm but her breath was forbidding. I couldn't tell whether she wanted me to come closer or to run away.

Hank Riley and Carol lingered a few paces behind me. I was under the impression they were trying to keep a safe distance. I'm not sure what they thought was going to happen.

I looked at my guardians. Carol squinted at me like a skeptic. Her lips were pursed and dry. Hank Riley offered a smile. His palms were out, facing up. His eyes were open and bright. He was receptive to this experience. He was receptive because he had hope. Contrarily, I suspected there was some part of Carol which sought to confirm for herself an innate badness of people like me. She could not conceive, herself, and so she held her own malady as a symbol of virtue.

"The monseigneur will see you now," the chubby woman said. I held my breath as I walked past her toward the barely cracked door. I edged the door open.

Sitting in a velveteen armchair was an unassuming man with spectacularly blue eyes. The blue was so vibrant it permanently penetrated my memory on first sight. I was sure, upon seeing his irises for the first time, I'd never forget him.

I didn't have an attraction to him so much as I felt an immediate magnetism toward the monseigneur. I could absolutely feel the distance between myself and this man as I stood in the doorway, experienced as electricity between us.

"Come in," he said.

I opened the door wider. He peered at Hank Riley and Carol in the background and then he looked at my face, studying it.

"Let's speak alone this first time," he suggested. I turned my head to see if Hank Riley agreed and my guardians were already nodding, waving me onward.

I shut the door behind me. The sunlight came in through the thick glass windows in a soft, warm glow. It cast shadows everywhere.

I felt electricity undulate as I walked across the office toward the armchair opposite the monseigneur. Sitting under his gaze, I understood how people might come to believe in God through this man.

The monseigneur was silent for a long time before he finally remarked, "You're not uncomfortable with silence."

I shook my head. I didn't really see why I should be discomforted by people not talking.

"It's unusual," he said.

"Why?"

"People want to fill silence. They'll reveal their hand, so to speak." The monseigneur folded his own hands neatly in his lap. "You don't."

I looked at the portrait of Jesus above his desk. The man had a crown of thorns and was in agony. It seemed like a brutal portrait to see every day as you went to work.

"There was something about the letter you wrote, Suzanne, that made me feel as though you are seeking something. Something more than what this world can offer," he said.

I noticed the places in the painting where the grisly thorns breached Jesus's skin and caused small spots of blood. It must have been painful. I never understood why Jesus did what he did in the stories and all. I never really got what the point of it all was. It seemed like a lot of pain and for what? The world was still a shithole.

"You're interested in the Savior? The Son of God?" he asked, noticing the direction of my gaze.

"Not really," I said, and it was true enough. Martyrs were wasted on women like Mama; they were wasted on men like Milton.

"Have you ever prayed, Suzanne?" the monseigneur asked.

"Yep," I said.

"What did you feel when you prayed?" he probed. I tried not to look at his eyes. They were piercing. They were the type of eyes that could get straight to your soul. I didn't think I had a soul anymore. And if I did, I wasn't sure I wanted anyone to see it; it was probably blackened and diseased. Like the lungs of a lifelong smoker, I had the soul of a lifelong sinner.

"I prayed when I was little," I began. "I didn't really know how. My mama never showed me. I had a dog and his name was Moses. I was real into this idea of God and Jesus, Moses and Noah. My friend, she told me all about all of them."

The monseigneur's right index finger rubbed the top of his other hand. Otherwise, he remained completely still.

"Anyway, it's not worth getting into all the details. Mama's dead, so what's the use? But there was a time when Moses needed somebody like Jesus. Or God. Or Noah to take him away on a ship somewhere safe. And I prayed." I felt a long-lost lump in my throat. I tried to suppress it, but the more I tried to make it go away, the more pronounced it felt.

All I saw through the shadows were the monseigneur's blue eyes. They held me in thrall. I didn't want to say more, but the machine had begun and could not stop until the process was finished. My words were outside of my control. Something long forgotten had begun to make my heart weep once again. It hurt.

"I prayed on my knees by my bed because that's how I saw in the picture books when I was little. I prayed to God. And I prayed to Jesus," I said, gesturing to the portrait of the martyr on the wall. "I said to them, if you save my Moses, if you save my dog, I will do anything for you. I said I will be your best friend. I said I will be your slave. I pleaded. I cried. I tore a few pieces of my hair out and pinched my arm real hard."

To demonstrate, I pinched my own arm until a red splotch appeared. The monseigneur listened in silence as his right index finger kept stroking his palm.

"And none of those men, little fairy tales that they are, answered me. Or maybe I'm not good enough for them," I said. I laughed a dry, hollow laugh. "In any case, my Moses was sweet, he was, and so even if I was bad, why did he have to die? If there's such a thing as God, he never, ever has ever shown me any love. But then again, who am I? My mother didn't love me and my father wanted me for parts. So who am I to God? I think he's likely made my value quite clear."

The monseigneur softly beckoned, "Suzanne, look at me."

My eyes, ringed with water of memories past, looked into his. His face was calm, and I could not sense him concealing any ulterior intent.

"Death isn't a bad thing," he said. His voice was confident and even, just above a whisper, as if he were passing along a beloved secret of the universe.

The armchair felt bigger than it had when I'd first entered and the light all but faded from the office. I stared into his blue eyes and asked, "How can you be so sure? You know, there are men and women who go door-to-door and they are passionate and loud, and they tell you that God is real with a fierce fire. And you—you sit there like you're doing a damn crossword and you tell me death isn't a bad thing. Have you ever seen death? Do you know whose sister I am?" I realized I'd screamed the last question.

The chubby woman rapped on the door, "Is everything alright?"

"We're fine, Martha," the monseigneur called out. Even his words of authority were poised.

"I know whose sister you are." He did not sound afraid.

"I could have him call someone. I could have him tell someone from the inside who's getting out to come out here and murder you in your sleep. Then would you sit there and think 'Death isn't a bad thing?'"

The monseigneur took this time to stare at his hands. He studied them as if he hadn't known them his whole life. He had an astounding disinterest in my anger.

"There's an old man I serve named Mr. Lorry. He lives alone with his three dogs and he's having trouble caring for them. I've prayed on it and I think you might be of service to him."

This caught me off guard. I wasn't used to people responding to anger so calmly. I had just threatened to kill the man. I didn't understand why he would trust me with a favor.

I squirmed in my seat. I kind of wanted to leave, but I was also intrigued. "What kind of dogs?" I asked.

The monseigneur looked up at me. There was a smile on his face. "German Shepherds. All three of them female."

17

MILTON, SPORTING A sly grin, came by Mr. Jack's that Tuesday.

"What's got you so happy?" I asked, though I wasn't keen to talk. I was in a bit of a malaise, I guess you could say. Hank Riley and Carol really wanted me to take the monseigneur up on his offer to go help Mr. Lorry. When I told them I already had a job, they then offered to pay me a wage equivalent to working at the hot dog stand if I helped Mr. Lorry instead.

Milton wrapped his arms around my waist and pressed up behind me. My hand went for the paring knife I had used on the tomatoes. Instinct took over.

Milton felt hard against me. One of his hands slipped inside my work pants. As his fingers got to the crest of my pubic hair, I realized that if he fucked me then and there, I'd take it for the time.

And after that—I'd kill him.

I'd fucking kill him, I thought, as the cold pads of his greasy fingers slid deeper and downward.

Then, finally, he stopped.

Good for him, I thought.

He whispered in my ear, "Girl, I'm just having fun with you."

The wretch took his time backing off. When I turned around, he had sex in his eyes and a hand on his crotch. My breasts were his favorite thing. I should've cut the things off and given them to him come Christmas.

"You're an asshole," I said and he laughed.

"None more an asshole than your brother."

"What's Lim got to do with you being an asshole?" I asked.

I kept the knife in my hand and held Milton squarely in my vision. Truth be told, I would've had a hard time killing Milton. He was a mean, scrappy fellow and I could read all over his face the restraint it took for him not to have his way.

I never told Hank Riley or Carol about Milton. I wanted to keep hearing anything I could about my brother. I did not believe in God, but I sometimes wondered if there weren't a strange karmic currency at play. In recompense for still having some semblance of family, an evil girl like myself had to pay. I told myself that sometimes when Milton took out his dick and stroked it at Mr. Jack's.

I told myself I deserved it.

It reminded me of times with Mama. It reminded me of worse times with some of Mama's friends. I may have seen men die and I may have helped men die, but whenever Milton took out his cock, I froze up like I was a kid or something. I couldn't explain it if I tried.

There were those papers they handed out at school that told you different ways you could say no. I had studied that guide many times over. I had worn out the paper so much it had started to fray at the edges. I was entranced by that idea—that a word could have power.

I was entranced by the idea a word could keep me safe.

I am sure there was a time in my life when I had said *no*—when I had said *please, no*—when I had tried to walk away. There was a time I had said and done all the things to express I did not want what had happened to me. I could not tell you the exact time the power of *no* was beaten out of me, but I did not know how to say it anymore.

I could bash, I could cut and I could run if I had to. I could do the things I needed to to keep breathing. But when Milton took out his dick and forced me to watch, I could not even utter the word *no*. All I could do was stare and hurt, a frozen bruise of a woman.

Certain memories emerged whenever men or women made sexual gestures at me. I always felt like my body was up for grabs. I didn't want to have it anymore. I wanted to cut out all of the entrances. I wanted to shut my body down. If there were an option to sew myself up forever I would've taken it. I was certain there was no worse feeling than having someone inside of you when you did not want it. It did not go away. The memory raped long after the person stopped. My childhood self was clay and sometimes I felt like my insides were shaped by their fingers, by their organs, by their wills. I didn't even want to touch myself, or look at it, really. I didn't want anything to do with it except to maybe cut it out of me.

Milton groaned at his climax and came into a napkin. He crumpled it up and threw it on the floor. He was gross like that.

"One day, I'm going to fuck your throat raw," he said breathily.

I turned back to the condiments and busied my hands, though my mind felt scattered.

"I don't think I'll be working here anymore," I said.

I could hear Milton stir behind me. "You don't work here, you won't hear about your brother," he played.

18

IT WAS A long drive to Mr. Lorry's house. The rural landscape we hit reminded me of my trip with Lim. I couldn't help but think of Lena and her secrets.

"What's going on in that big brain of yours, Suzy?" Hank Riley asked, an absurdly chipper smile on his face. He had an impenetrable optimism about him and, though I was reluctant to admit it, sometimes I felt scared for Hank Riley. Men like him didn't stand a chance.

"I'm thinking about Lim."

As soon as the words came out, I regretted them. Hank Riley's personal mission was to get me to view my brother as an enemy.

Today, though, he seemed pensive. His manicured fingers strummed the steering wheel, his face pinched as he looked at the passing road. "What about him?" he asked. There was no discernible judgment in his voice.

"Just thinking about the drive we took, is all. There was one part of it that looked like this. Country."

"Did you ever get to go out places and see the world before then? Did you travel, I mean?"

"Not really. Pretty much hung around Morris Grove," I replied.

"Well I'm really proud of you that you're going to help Mr. Lorry for the monseigneur. I know you don't want to." Hank Riley took his eyes off the road for a second. His eyes were kind. The way he looked at me made me uncomfortable. My discomfort wasn't because he wanted anything, but precisely because I felt like he wanted nothing. It was easier to deal with people when I could see the blueprint of their desires.

As we pulled up to Mr. Lorry's house, I felt anxious. I didn't know how to do good and felt unsure of why I had said yes. Part of me felt like maybe if I helped someone, maybe I could make up for some of it. Be someone different, Suzy, I told myself. Be less like you.

The car parked.

"That must be them," Hank Riley said.

I followed his gaze and saw three German shepherds lying on the porch.

"Where's the old man?" I asked.

"He must be inside. The monseigneur said he's really ill," Hank Riley responded.

We both got out of the car with caution. I knew German Shepherds were very territorial, but these three girls just lay on the porch, side-eyeing me. I guessed that since there were three of them, they didn't consider me much of a threat.

They each had golden and black fur, their tongues flopping out of their mouths with that even, rhythmic panting dogs did on hot days. There was a musculature to their bodies I admired. I wished my own body could gleam so tautly beneath my fine hair. I'd replace my breasts with their lean flanks if I could.

The dogs had real presence. They were calm, but I sensed a readiness on their part to attack at any moment. They were three beasts which commanded my respect almost immediately.

Hank Riley rapped on the screen door. There was no answer so he edged it open a little.

"Mr. Lorry?" he called out.

I sat down next to one of the shepherds. She had one solid black ear and one solid brown ear. I gently ran my palm across her side. She lifted her head and looked at me.

She and I stared into each other's blackness, searching for intent. Could we trust each other? Would I hurt her, or would she bite me? I stroked her side ever-so-lightly with my hand and thought about the world for a moment and all the people in it.

There were people who hurt others thinking others would hurt them. And then there were people who hurt others knowing others wouldn't hurt them back. The world was all comprised of people just causing hurt.

And it got me to thinking for a moment about love and what does love mean. And I wanted to ask Hank Riley this important question, but there was something about his beige sandals and the way his shorts fell, the dopiness of his haircut and the sincerity of his gaze as he poked around for Mr. Lorry . . .

Instead, I stared into that girlish beast's eyes, the shepherd of the house. And the darkness of her pupils told me everything I'd ever already supposed about life.

Finally, there was a rustle from inside and the screen door popped open with a creak.

Mr. Lorry was in his seventies, his skin sickly looking with jaundice. Ragged tufts of gray hair twirled off his mottled scalp in bizarre, frayed curls. He rested his weight uneasily on a robust cane.

The shepherds became more alert in the old man's presence. One, with a black oval on her back, went to his side and sat on her haunches. Her tongue was flapping like a good girl, but I wasn't fooled. I was sure she would go right for my throat if I had ill intent. I surmised they were smart beasts and I took a liking to them right off.

Mr. Lorry, on the other hand, didn't seem terribly impressed with me, though I could hardly blame him.

"They sent a girl?" was the first question out of the old man's mouth.

It was an odd moment. Hank Riley looked over at me and I thought I caught him glancing at my breasts. I had to wonder, did he just realize I was a woman? He shifted dopily in his sandals.

"They told me they were going to send a boy," Mr. Lorry continued.

"Well, I guess this isn't going to work out then," I said and took a few steps to leave the porch. Hank Riley stopped me with an outstretched arm.

"Well, Mr. Lorry, this is Suzy and I think—*no, I know*—she is going to be wonderful with your dogs. Suzy is a huge help around the house for me and my wife, Carol."

"If the church recommended her, she can't be all that much of a help," the old man said with a hollow but booming laugh.

There was a moment of quiet and then the shepherd next to the old man did something I'd never understand. She walked over to me and licked my hand. Her lukewarm tongue lapped at my fingers. She finally took a seat next to me and stared at her master with an air of defiance. Or maybe I was imagining things.

The old man's face took on a fresh glance as he appraised the situation anew. "But if Clotho likes you, then I can't turn you away, now can I?"

"Clotho?" I asked.

"Clotho, Lachesis, and Atropos," he said, gesturing to each of the dogs. "The three fates. Girl, don't you read?"

Hank Riley, ever helpful, mentioned, "Suzy has been in and out of school for a bit, so she's catching up—"

"I do read actually," I interrupted.

Mr. Lorry took a step toward me, his heavy cane thumping against the porch wood. "What on God's earth you spending your time reading, that you don't know who the fates are?"

"I read murder magazines," I said.

"Suzy!" Hank Riley exclaimed. He seemed genuinely embarrassed of me or maybe for me or both. I couldn't really make it out but the man was head-to-toe ashamed.

The old man waved a hand at my tepid ward. "It's alright. I get the allure of those rags. But don't you know there's plenty of murder in classic literature, too?"

I hadn't really thought about it.

"What kind of murder?"

"All kinds, girl. Torture, rape, murder. Deceit! The deceit is what will get you," he said, wagging a finger in the air. "To come in as a murderer and to murder is one thing. To come in as a friend, but to be a foe is another. Deceit is really the true crime of humanity."

Hank Riley faded into the periphery. He didn't seem to understand this interaction and, for a moment, I could see on his face the semblance of regret for taking me here. Maybe he was thinking he was wrong about me or maybe he was wrong about this old man or maybe the church. He was not a confident man, that Hank Riley. He lurched awkwardly throughout his life on the path he thought was good but he was never really sure if the good path was worthwhile.

"Well. So, are you a friend, or are you a foe?" Mr. Lorry asked. He looked me straight in the eye.

"How can I know that yet? We've only just met," I answered.

As Hank Riley took a step away from me, the old man took a step forward. There was glee in his eyes and he laughed in a way that was solid and deep, surprising for his apparent physical frailty.

"Now that's an honest girl," he said to Hank Riley and then he opened the door to his house.

Like all good monsters, I came not by force, but by invitation.

19

MILTON WAS IN a foul mood when I told him I was leaving Mr. Jack's for good.

"Bobby will take over my shifts," I said, referring to Mr. Jack's nephew. Bobby was a lanky, acne-faced youth who liked to talk about his action figure collection.

"Bobby can go suck a dick," Milton sneered into his bottle. There was a rank odor about him, like he hadn't washed in a week.

"Shit, he can suck mine," he continued, nursing whatever foul liquor he was drinking. The paper bag crinkled in his thick-fingered grip.

"What's got you so angry?" I asked, though I didn't particularly care.

Milton shoved off the bottle and leaned back in his chair. With his head to the ceiling and his legs splayed wide, he began to tell me about his evening.

"I've been working at that damn mill for three months and they let me go like that," he said. He snapped his fingers for effect. There was flame in his eyes.

"Why'd they let you go?"

"What do you mean, why they let me go? You ain't dumb, you know how it is. These guys, they don't give a flying fuck."

I stared at him, waiting for the real reason.

"Alright, so . . ." he began. He paused to drain the last of his bottle before tossing it in the trash. "Look, I was with my boys minding my business and one of these guys, we call him Toots, found a stray cat. One of them calicos, walking along."

I already knew the rest of the story, as if I'd heard it a million times over. As if it were encoded in my genes before I had been born.

"Anyway, we just had us a good time. Toots took the thing by her tail and she was clawing and scratching. Boy," he laughed, "you wouldn't believe how one of them things screams when she knows what's coming to her."

I believed.

"What happened to her?" I asked.

Milton laughed like a little boy. "Threw the bitch in the fire. Howled like a motherfucker, too."

Milton stood up and came close to me. He leaned in and took me in his arms, his mouth close to my ear. The alcohol on his breath was strong enough to make me tipsy secondhand. "You ever see a roasted pussy, little girl?"

His thick fingers caressed my midsection. The thought of the dead cat was turning him on.

"I've seen worse," I said and my thoughts scattered. I saw Moses and I saw the legless pig. I remembered it squirming and writhing in the mud. I could hear its railing squeals as Milton pinched my nipple under my shirt. He pinched it so hard it hurt and I hated myself then because despite how much I hated him, my body still responded to his touch. I felt like a toy in his hands waiting to be broken. The best I could hope for was to be tossed aside.

"You wanna go on a ride with me?" he asked.

"My shift's not over."

"Fuck your shift," he said with a laugh.

We locked up Mr. Jack's. I wasn't sure why I was going with Milton except for the fact that something about the way he talked and moved felt like home. I didn't like it and I didn't want it, but it called to me. I played the dog and as I followed Milton to his car, I thought of Clotho, Lachesis, and Atropos. I thought of their muscular, powerful bodies and their beautiful, long snouts.

And I thought of their yellowed, sturdy teeth.

I played the dog to any master who'd have me, I supposed, as I got into Milton's car. We rattled off down the main highway and took a few side turns until we got to a road I'd never been on before. I morbidly considered I might never return.

I hung my head out the window, letting the breeze smack some energy into me. I knew, as long as we kept on driving, I'd be okay. It was when we'd stop that I'd have to worry.

"I'm thinking of getting outta this place," Milton said as he pulled into a dirt emergency pull-off. Some dust skittered up by my window and I took a look around. I wasn't familiar with the area. There was nothing in sight except trees.

"Where are you gonna go?" I asked.

"I was thinking Florida. There's sun. Beaches. That great seafood shit. And tons of old bastards who need help spending their money."

Milton laughed then. I looked at his eyes—they were little and black. I'd seen the kind before. On snakes and other slithering things.

He reclined in his seat and put his hands behind his head.

"There's a lick of somethin' in the glovebox if you want to take the edge off."

I shook my head and slumped against the passenger side door.

"Milton," I said, and his dark gaze shifted over to me with maybe, just maybe, a flicker of interest. "Do you ever get bored?"

Milton laughed. "I'm bored like a motherfucker. Shit, I thought about fucking you up right here," he said as his eyes darted to my thighs and back to my face, "but then I felt too lazy to try."

I ignored the threat. Men like Milton fed off fear and discomfort. "I get bored, too. All the time. Even so, I feel like I should be bored, right? Like that's the good life, being able to be bored? Except, even when things are bad, really bad, I still feel that boredom."

"It's 'cause they beat your heart out of you. They beat it out of me, too. Now we're just crocodiles, like, and no one can tell the difference. I'll tell you something. My pa, he was a sonuvabitch."

Milton reached into the glovebox and pulled out a flask. He emptied whatever was left into his mouth and tossed it back.

"A real sonuvabitch." He let out a belch and closed his eyes as if he were remembering the man in that moment. "I remember my mom—and my mom was a fucking saint. Pathetic how much of a saint she was. She came home one night and she had this cough she'd picked up at work. It was a bad one. She coughed so much she threw up on the kitchen floor. And you know what that piece of shit did?"

I didn't have to answer.

"He made her eat it. Said if she didn't eat it, he was going to beat 'that boy.' That's what he called me, 'that boy.' Not his boy, not Milton, just 'that boy.' And fuck, I was named after the guy."

"That's horrible," I said, though my voice sounded flatter than I knew it should have.

"I guess it is. Makes him a sonuvabitch, that's for sure. Makes her an idiot. You women are all idiots and whores. And now before you go taking offense, just know I don't hold it against you."

Milton flashed a strange smile at me—a smile that would've passed as charisma to a certain type of prey on a barstool. His eyes were blacker than they'd looked moments previous.

"Your mom sounds nice, at least," I said. I couldn't have imagined my own mother doing the same. If anything, Mama would have enjoyed seeing me get beat. She often played that game without any prompting.

"Yeah, sure. She was nice. Idiots and whores are often nice," he reasoned.

"Your parents still alive?" I asked.

"Sure are. Live in the same damn trailer park I was born in," he said. "And before you go asking, because you chicks always ask, no we don't have Christmas together." He laughed again, a hollow laugh.

Milton then pulled out his dick and started stroking himself. As much as I wanted to look away, I knew there'd be trouble if I did.

I deserved this. I wasn't any better than Milton just because Hank Riley gave me soft sheets to sleep in now. I watched until he came with a long, raspy groan. He zipped up his pants without even cleaning himself off and stared at me, his predatory gaze somehow sharpened.

"So. Tell me about this old man they got you watching dogs for."

For the first time in a long time, I felt a twinge of fear.

20

CAROL CAME INTO my room that night. A towel was wrapped around her hair and her delicate, fair skin looked freshly scrubbed. She was cozy in a plush bathrobe. I looked down at her feet and saw her perfectly manicured nails covered with unblemished pink polish. Carol was everything I could never be.

"I wanted to say good night," she said, trying a smile. I knew how I looked. She was Barbie and I was something you'd find at a thrift store. Something dirty and damaged. I wasn't comfortable around Carol. I felt like she could see the ugliness inside of me.

"Good night," I said. I thought I was being polite, but I could see that my words hurt her. Her smile quaked as if she were fighting tears.

"Suzy, you know you can talk to me, right?" she asked.

I wondered if Hank Riley had put her up to this. Men tried to squeeze the women in their lives together, as if our common biology were enough to bond us. That's what men never understood about women. It wasn't enough just to have breasts to want to be together. We had minds, too. Men never saw the minds. They saw lumps and mounds, holes and crevasses. Places to stare, places to molest. Men were handsy that way. Tactile.

I nodded and stared past her. I didn't know what to say to a woman who painted her toenails and plucked every stray eyebrow hair.

"Okay, well, sweet dreams," she said. Her voice was faint and sad.

21

I WATCHED MR. LORRY from my favorite chair in the kitchen. His house was a hodgepodge of old furniture, stacks of papers, books, and memorabilia. There was charm and security to the clutter. He had built a fortress from his possessions.

The old man tottered at the counter with a metal thermos. He pulled out two ceramic mugs from the cabinet, all while leaning precariously on his cane. The gray tufts at the sides of his head were especially unruly this morning, curling and twirling in various directions.

"What's in the thermos?" I asked.

"Goat's milk," he responded.

I probably made a face because he quickly chastised me. "It's healthier than cow's milk. A woman from church brings it to me."

"A woman?" I asked. It was hard to think of Mr. Lorry having any romantic interests. Oddly, scattered about his house and amidst the piles of clutter, there were no hints of anything beyond the material. He didn't even own photos of his three dogs, who at the moment lounged about his feet, lazily watching for the cane's trajectory.

The old man caught the nuance of my question and didn't find it at all amusing. He poured the goat's milk into a saucepan and turned on the gas. Next, he pulled out a chocolate bar from the fridge and broke it up into pieces into the pan.

"This is how she used to make it," he said.

I wanted to pry but also thought myself unworthy of knowing more about his life. I'd been there three Saturdays now and mostly he had me sit at the dining room table and work on a puzzle or two with him.

Sometimes he'd read aloud the crossword hints and I'd tell him, as usual, that I was terrible at those. He always said I had to try harder to get better at them, but any time he handed over one to me, I'd fill out three rows and have to quit. He'd dutifully take over and finish every last column. He used those erasable pens, the types that write in really faded black ink. He said they were a tremendous invention of mankind.

Mr. Lorry set down a mug of the goat's milk hot chocolate in front of me. I was nervous to try it. I thought of Lena and wondered if she would enjoy it. I thought of her soft, round belly. I thought of how a mug of this would have done her good. I stared down at the thick chocolatey substance and a sudden sadness overwhelmed me. It surprised me hard, like one of Mama's smacks to the head.

I felt silly and ashamed because Lena was dead and her baby was dead, too. This hot chocolate wasn't going to do them any good; it was going to sit and warm my ungrateful monstrous belly, a belly that didn't hold a baby. A belly that held nothing but a monster's intestines. I wished someone would just rip them out already and put me out of my misery.

"Try it," Mr. Lorry goaded.

I brought the mug to my lips. The steam hit my nose and it smelled really good. It made me feel like I was in a Christmas commercial.

I let it touch my lips and then put it back down. It was much too hot.

"That's how she liked it," he said. His lips curled into something that was probably once a smile. Now it looked broken.

I stared intently at the puzzle box set out for today. The picture on the front showed a train going through a valley during sunset.

Mr. Lorry shook the pieces out of the box and onto the table.

"Have you ever been on a train?" he asked.

I shook my head and brought the mug to my lips again. I took a sip and let the hot chocolate ease over my tongue and down my throat. It tasted and felt odd . . . perhaps loving.

"Never been on a train? Really now," the old man repeated aloud, scanning all the pieces on the table. He nabbed a corner piece and set it off to the side. It was his way of doing things—to grab the corners first.

"Have you?" I asked.

"Not in a long time."

"What's it like?"

I took another drink. The mug warmed my hands. I slouched a little in my chair and looked at Clotho, who had curled herself by my feet. She was a giant mass of muscle making herself vulnerable near me. I reached down and patted her head. She barely moved; she wasn't scared of me. I wondered at that—shouldn't she be?

"A train lets you be alone with your thoughts. It takes you along at the right speed. A plane—that's a different matter. A plane wants to rush things. It jumbles your soul and makes everything come out much too fast. There's no time to think on a plane. But on a train, you can actually have a thought that might matter in the end."

I didn't really understand what Mr. Lorry was going on about, but I liked to hear his voice. It was low and assertive. Past where he sat, I could see through the window into his backyard where two birds chipped away at a seed-block. I kept putting the mug to my lips and patting the dog's head, listening to the old man and looking out at the peaceful yard. I didn't want to like the place as much as I did. I didn't even want to be capable of liking it because that meant it could be taken from me. Nothing could stop a man from taking if he wanted it.

"Where are you from, Suzy?"

I took another drink to give myself a moment before I had to answer. I thought to lie, but then I just told him. "I'm from Morris Grove."

"Morris Grove? Never heard of it."

"No one has, really. Small town . . . I lived with my mama and brother, Lim."

The old man looked up at me. "Ah. Yes. I've heard your story. I read it in the papers."

"The papers didn't say everything."

Mr. Lorry stopped working on the puzzle and slid back in his chair.

I continued, "There was another side to my brother. And the papers, they say he kidnapped me. Lim didn't. Lim never hurt me. He didn't make me go with him. I went with him willingly. I wanted to."

I took the mug to my lips again, but realized the hot chocolate was all gone. I set down the empty mug and looked for Clotho but she, too, had disappeared. The old man stared at me hard.

"You should read more," he said finally, and again turned his attention to the puzzle.

I felt slighted by his dismissal. He didn't seem at all interested in knowing more about Lim or Mama—or me. All he was interested in was assembling that cheap picture of a train at sunset.

He'd never ride another train, I thought, and suddenly I found him pathetic in his old house, surrounded by his life's possessions. He was alone and picking at painted cardboard jigsaw pieces.

"I do read. I read *True Crime.* One day, you know, they'll put an article in there about Lim."

"And you, you want to say," the old man muttered.

"And me. Sure."

I watched him. I wanted him to care, I realized. I wanted to provoke him. I hated how he could ignore my entire life and wave it away. What did he know about human suffering?

"No one's going to care about your brother, girl."

"He's one of the coldest killers out there. They said so."

"It does make for a nice headline and papers need to sell. So does the nightly news."

"There's no one else in the world like Lim. And he'd do anything to keep me safe."

The old man laughed and my face burned hot at his mockery. I wanted to grab his cane and throttle him about his laughing head. Instead, I raised a hand and swiped half the puzzle off the table. The pieces went flying. Lachesis perked her head up from across the kitchen and bared her teeth at me, a very soft growl growing.

I stood up and readied for a confrontation. I knew Mr. Lorry would want to be rid of me eventually.

"Lim would kill you dead if he heard you laughing at me like that."

"Sit down," Mr. Lorry said, his voice sounding more tired than anything else.

I was surprised he didn't sound angry. I was more surprised he didn't tell me to leave. I sat down and waited.

"You've been over here several times. I like you. You're a bright young lady," the old man began. He turned his head away from me. "You remind me of my daughter—when you're not acting foolish."

"I didn't know you had a daughter."

"Have. She's dead but she's still mine."

Mr. Lorry stood up and walked to the sink. He twisted the knob on—then off—then on again. He next went to a cabinet and opened it. He looked for seemingly nothing, shuffled around a few glasses and closed it again. It was as if he were lost in his own house. He finally let his weight fall back on his cane and slumped into himself.

"It's very easy to destroy, Suzy. It's easy to tear things apart." He gestured to the puzzle pieces all across the kitchen floor. "How easily you destroyed the puzzle. The pieces are everywhere now and the picture that could have been—isn't."

I got down on the floor and started picking up the pieces.

"No. Sit," he said. I looked up at him, confused. "This is important. You have to understand this."

"Understand what?"

"That even though it feels like God to kill another human being, you are the opposite of God. Every foul word you speak about another person, every item you soil, every person you harm. That is not the work of a God, but of a maggot." A palm outstretched, as if summoning God, himself, to testify.

He continued, "And this world has lots of maggots. They multiply and feed on the vulnerable as though it were their natural right. Your brother is a maggot. And you, hell. You might be one, too. Who am I to say?"

I wanted to feel angry. I looked at my hands and studied the dirt gathered around the cuticle beds. My eyes welled and I tried to fend off the wave inside of me.

"My wife and daughter were taken by the maggots. The destroyers. Maybe you've read about it in your true crime rag. And what's it worth to you to read the sordid details? They said my daughter was still alive, blood pumping to her heart, when they—" and his voice cracked. His spine seemed to break in four places, his posture was so odd, so overcome with grief was he. The agony that poured from his flesh flooded my own and I found myself on my knees looking for something.

But I knew there was no God. There could not be a God.

"I'm so sorry that happened to you," I said. At least I thought I'd said it. I thought the words, but I was so paralyzed with the old man's sorrow that it's possible I remained silent. It struck me that his sorrow was mightier than mine. There was something sacred about his anger, as if he had let it ferment over time. It was potent.

"The men who did it laughed at trial. They whistled. They looked at me and smiled. So easy was it to destroy . . . so easy was it. They took what my wife and I had built over sixteen years, sacrificing and toiling every day from love, and inside of an hour, reduced it to ash. And you can read about them. You can be like them."

His eyes glowed as he leaned down and stared into my own. I thought he might strike me. I wanted him to strike me. I deserved it.

"But for every one of your brother's kind and for every one of your kind if you wish it, there are Builders, and there are Creators. In the end, they will see Him. They will see the Kingdom of Heaven and you will be alone floating in the darkness. You will see a light on the horizon and no matter how long you float in your filth, you will never reach it. That will be your punishment—to see a Paradise you cannot ruin."

22

I NEVER WANTED to get too comfortable in Hank Riley's house. I sometimes devised ways I might control my own departure, so sure was I that they'd send me packing at one point sooner than later.

It was storming outside and I slouched around the kitchen watching Carol cook. She pounded chicken breasts with a metal mallet. She did it delicately and with a steady rhythm. It was a slow and tender beating. Next she took out cheese and prosciutto, and rolled them up in the thin, beaten breasts.

Carol periodically looked over her left shoulder at me with a forced half smile trying to conceal her uneasiness.

"I should have had you beat the chicken. It's kind of fun," she said. When I didn't answer, she suppressed her nerves with a swig of white wine. The thunder howled outside. An occasional burst of lightning shone through the pale shade drawn over the window.

There was a hue to the room that reminded me of being back home with Lim and Mama. Mama used to bake sometimes. There were dollar store mixes where you could just mix in milk or an egg and bake for thirty minutes or so. I remembered lining muffin pans and feeling so accomplished. The little papers came in pastels and Mama would let me line the pans with them.

I hated having positive memories about Mama because they filled me with dread only one of my kind could know. They made me feel gross from the inside. The positive memories made me feel like I enjoyed the bad stuff. And it was so hard because I couldn't have a positive memory without the bad stuff riding in close behind. If I could tell a parent one thing, it would be this: you can be the best damn parent in the world Monday through Saturday but if you hit your kid on Sunday, that's all the kid will remember. Your hand and the hurt, the anger in your eyes.

I always remembered Mama's hands. I rarely remembered baking muffins.

"What are you thinking about?" Carol asked. Half of her hair was pinned back with the hair in the front set in soft curls around her face. I never understood how she found the time to be so perfect and how she could be so happy about spending so much of her life on it.

"Nothing," I lied. She did the thing again—where she looked hurt by the sound of my voice.

"Why do you do that?" I shot back this time.

She set the mallet down and looked at me, confused. "Do what?"

"You look hurt every time I speak. I've never seen someone as delicate as you."

She looked even more hurt at that, which I didn't even think was possible. "I care, is all," she said, a tad indignant. She turned back to the mallet. I watched her hand reach for it.

"It feels good, doesn't it?" I said. "To beat that chicken."

"It does," she relented, her shoulders rising in anxiety.

"It felt good when I did it to a human. That's how I know. Never did it to a chicken, though."

"Suzy, stop."

"You know that about me, right? Did they tell you?"

"Suzy!" she yelled, her voice rising.

A clap of thunder erupted outside. I reached for the mallet at the same time she did. Our fingers touched each other's as they both grappled for the metal. I yanked it from her pale, slender hand.

A wave of terror spread across her face as I backed her into the corner of the kitchen.

"Suzy," she said again, her voice this time soft and feeble, like the whimpering of a dying animal. I raised the mallet and she shrunk back from me. Her pale hands in front of her face were her only defense.

"Did they tell you what I did?" I asked again.

Carol shrunk down into a squat, her palms facing up. I felt her fear. I did not want to hurt Carol, but a part of me raged that she could be so weak and yet alive. That she could be so fragile and yet so sheltered. There was no evolution like they talked about in school. Because if there really were evolution, then it would be me who had what Carol had, and Carol? She would've been dead already.

My senses were heightened. I thought of Mama next to me, telling me I had stirred the muffin batter good. "You did good, Suzy," she'd said.

But she'd said it at other times, too. Bad times.

I threw the mallet across the room. It fell with a loud clank before sliding across the floor. I slid down against the cabinets.

"I can understand if you have to kick me out now. I know I can't live here anymore," I said. I held my head in my hands and tried to hear the sound of the rain outside. I wanted to get lost in its rhythm. Only, the rain had stopped. The only sound was Carol's sobs.

I knew, at a time like this, that one was supposed to say, "I'm sorry," and though I could've easily said those words, I didn't. I didn't think anyone would've believed me.

We both heard the front door open. Carol deflated with relief as Hank Riley walked in, his hair dripping from the rain. He carried an absurd pink umbrella that could only have belonged to his wife. As sad a scene as Carol and I were, crouched and speechless, Hank Riley was somehow more sad in his business casual attire, slouchy posture, and rain-smeared spectacles.

The suburban husband seemed awfully unresponsive to the atmosphere of the room, which surprised me. I'd half a thought that something bad happened and was about to break the silence when Hank Riley did it for me.

The words poured from his mouth as though he were trying to get them out as quickly as possible.

"Suzy, Lim's dead," he said with one breathless muttering.

My eyes focused in on the floor before me, which opened up like the sky. My mind wandered across every stray crumb, every fallen hair, and every crack in the tile. I started to hallucinate designs with the ephemera.

As I stared at a curled strand of my own hair, which lay partially beneath my right foot—a hair that looked too much like Mama's—I remembered a time, after one of Mama's railings, when Lim had come into my room. In the dark blue light of night, Lim, my giant brother, my archangel, had come to save me. He had opened the window and removed the screen. Though I had been unable to see his expression in the moonlight, I had felt him staring and willing me on.

"Go," he had said, and he had laid a thick wad of cash on the window sill. "You might have to do bad things sometimes, but sometimes you have to do bad to get good."

When he had left my room, it had felt like a mirage. I could still recall the exact feel of that night's breeze on my bruised skin. I had known things weren't going to get much better, after all, but as I had started to climb my dresser to fit through the window, it was Alice's voice that had stopped me.

"Don't leave me," she pleaded. Her voice had sounded so soft and sad. I had let the fresh air wash over my face. I was sure I had looked like a ghost in the night, a lost soul staring out and jealous of all who lived.

I hadn't left Morris Grove that night. And maybe I should have.

But it was Lim who had opened the window and who had shown me the way. It was I who had turned to my magazine and who had run my fingers one more time over the photo of the dead blonde. Unlike Lim, I wasn't doing bad to get good.

I *was* bad.

When my eyes lifted from that rogue dark hair, I saw Carol mopping up what could only be my vomit. I had messed all over my shirt and the floor. There were chunks of hot dog from my shift at Mr. Jack's reappearing undigested in yellow bile.

It was only then that I said, "I'm sorry," as I felt stupid for having thrown up in front of the two.

I stood to grab some paper towels but Hank Riley put his hand on my shoulder to stop me.

"Sit. It's okay," he said.

"How did he die?" I asked, trying not to look anywhere in particular. The kitchen swarmed around me like a blur.

No one answered my question, so I finally made myself look Hank Riley in the eye. There was something in his gaze, something he hadn't wanted to express, but it was hiding there. It was dark—darker than he would have liked.

"I don't think I should say. The advocate didn't even want me to tell you about his death. It's, uhh, it's . . ." he stumbled over the right word.

"Inadvisable for your recovery," Carol chimed in. Her voice was robotic. I looked down to see her losing herself in cleaning the floor. She had found something to focus on that didn't directly involve me and she thrust her attention at it with all her might. I was her husband's foolish idea, not hers. She was just being a good wife. Supportive, meek, a helpmate.

I leaned against the counter for support.

"All this time, you wouldn't let me see him. And now he's dead,"

I said.

Hank Riley reached out to touch me again, as if his hands could offer anything palliative. I didn't want to be touched and I shrugged him off. He looked wounded, like all men did when their touch was rejected. It was okay for me to be upset, so long as he could control it. My emotions weren't something to listen to or empathize with, but something to solve. Like a broken toilet in the middle of the night.

"I think I have a right to know how he died," I said again. I thought about Moses then, if only briefly. I thought about the feeling of his ribs beneath his soft, black fur. I thought about the mucus in his eyes. And the night when Lim and I played God to the suffering.

"The court feels differently, I'm afraid. You'll be old enough soon and I'm sure you'll find out on your own. Let's get you some rest."

Carol, ever helpful, chimed in, "I think this calls for something special for dinner. What do you think, Hank?"

"Sure, whatever Suzy wants. What do you want to eat, Suzy? We'll get you anything you like. You want ice cream for dinner? Tacos? You love tacos. You want tacos?"

I wanted to swat them both away from my sight like gnats on a windshield. Breathless and agonized, I could only mutter, "Tacos are fine."

23

HANK RILEY AND Carol didn't want me to go to my final shift at Mr. Jack's, but I wanted out of the house. They had become cloying and unbearable after the news of Lim's death. Carol hadn't even mentioned the mallet incident to Hank Riley and instead had taken to staring at me like I was a wounded dog.

I was tired of playing the dog for everyone all the time.

I was tired of being alone with my thoughts. I had always half thought, even though Lim had been sentenced to life imprisonment, that maybe one day he would get out and we would be reunited. I had thought about traversing the very same route we had taken when we left Morris Grove, only this time we wouldn't be on the run from anything. This time, we could stop and enjoy ourselves. I wanted to create happy memories with my brother.

Maybe it was the weakness inside me that wanted such a pointless thing as to be able to recall happy moments with him, but all of my moments with Lim were colored by Mama. She was everywhere in my memory's landscape, shading everything in with her own brush. There was no way to eradicate the thing that had made me, or him. And now Lim was gone, too. I'd never be able to recall a time when I just sat with him, brother and sister, not a worry on our minds, looking to a future full of hope. That was as real as Alice's voice in the moonlight, I figured.

The loneliness of my life was highlighted now by being surrounded by people who couldn't understand me but loved to look at me. It was with that in mind that I was happy to see Milton the day after Lim's death.

I could look to Milton for the ugly truth of a thing because, whether I liked him or not, he was of me and I was of him. We had come from the same place, just under a different name.

"I heard about your brother," he said and slid over a fifth of something cheap, the label torn off. I took a drink even though I didn't care to drink much. I figured whatever was next out of his mouth wasn't going to be good.

"How'd he die?" I asked and stared squarely at Milton's eyes. He stared back with a hint of a smile curling up on one side. The muscles in his face twitched as he tried to suppress his growing glee.

"You sure you wanna know?"

"He's my brother."

"Seems like, a group of 'em got him in his cell. Now how they got there, I don't know, but they got there, is all, and it wasn't good.

He fought—you know he did. And he lost. Shoved a broom handle up his ass, they did, and if he'd lived, he wouldn't have been much for human after the way they tore that thing into him. In any case, he's damn near unrecognizable by the time they finished, so it's said."

Milton reached for the fifth and as it was about to hit his lips, he instead offered it to me. I didn't want it, so he about downed a third of it himself. I wanted to feel the pain.

"My brother was raped?"

"Real bad. I don't know if he was when he was alive or after. Probably both! Imagine, a big guy like that, too."

Lim's rape pained me far more than my own.

"I don't see how," I said, my voice cracking. Ever since I had been a child, Lim had been unstoppable. There wasn't a single person who had ever been able to hurt me in the neighborhood and it was because of Lim. In my mind, he had been immortal. The pain of him being torn apart from the inside and beaten was too much for me to bear. It bore a hole in the pit of me and began eating away. I could feel teeth inside my stomach gnawing and chomping. The pain inside me wanted to hurt. My pain needed to feed.

"You ever hunt?" Milton asked. He slid into a folding chair on the other side of the hot dog shack. "Sometimes you get a big buck, right, and you're kind of happy. Because it's a big fucking buck. But at the same time, man, it's a *big fucking buck*. You know?"

I shook my head.

"Yeah, you feel your hand on those incredible antlers and you think, how could a creature this big and powerful die just like the rest of us?"

He kicked his feet up.

"But that's the beauty of this world, Suzy. Everyone can die. Idn't nothing someone can do to you that they can't die for later."

He laughed then and I saw Milton's eyes change as they had in the car that one afternoon after he'd finished jerking off.

"I'm gonna miss you, you know," he continued.

"I won't miss you," I said.

"Nah, you don't mean that. I'm the only one who sees you for who you are."

Milton got up and pressed himself against me from behind, as he liked to do. I could feel his dick grow hard against my ass.

"You're not a girl, Suzy. You're just a bitch."

He let out a howl of laughter as I turned around and pushed him off. He staggered back, his hands in the air, teeth showing in an ill-fitting grin.

"What're you gonna do now? Sic your ass-ripped brother's corpse on me?"

Where anger should've been, I felt emptiness.

All I could say was, "No. I'm going to leave here in two hours and never see you again."

"Oh that's right, you gonna go and hang out with that old man? What's his old cock taste like, huh? He give you money for that shit?"

I rolled my eyes and listened to Milton cackle. He was his own favorite comedian. He sat back down and a more serious expression on his face took hold.

"You know they say that old man Lorry's got money up there with them dogs."

"I never saw any money," I said, and it was true. All I'd ever seen at Mr. Lorry's were piles of unorganized possessions, things no one would really want or deem of value.

"You would say that 'cause you want it all to yourself," Milton surmised. "But how about we split it?"

"There's nothing to split!" I snapped. "There's nothing out there but old newspapers and books and crap. He doesn't have any money."

"He's gotta have some money. And you know the place. We could go out there, kill the old fart, and run off together."

I looked at Milton long and hard. He was serious in his proposal and if I didn't know him better, I might've thought there was a tenderness to his eyes, something asking and not telling.

I shook my head. "Leave the old man alone. He's got three dogs besides."

"Ah shit, you're so green to the world. It'd be cute if it wasn't so fucking stupid," he said with the anger of a man rejected. He drained the fifth of its last amber color, tossed it in the trash, and left Mr. Jack's without so much as a goodbye.

Though I hoped it would be the last I'd see of him, I felt a sadness all the same, as if my life's foundation had just floated away. There I was, a pile of parts in a hot dog shack. No one needed to kill me, I thought, because I already felt dead.

24

ALICE STARTED SHOWING up all over town. Her face was plastered on cheap flyer paper in smudged black and white ink that reminded me of the smoky haze in which I'd last seen her. Her parents were still looking for her, the flyer said. They missed her terribly. They begged anyone who knew anything to come forward.

I liked to look at the flyers. Sometimes if I looked long enough, Alice's black, inky lips moved and tried to speak to me. I knew it had to have been my imagination, but I could hear her voice, the same pitch as if she were still calling out to me through the air vent. She kept saying, "Take me home."

I'd stare at those flyers for hours on end. Hank Riley let me take the car to Mr. Lorry's now. Only I often didn't go see the old man or his dogs. Instead, I'd shift around town like a lost ghost. I knew eventually Mr. Lorry would tell the monseigneur and my cover would be blown. But I had a thought to leave before then, either by my hand or open road.

I'd walk the main street up and down, fishweaving in between shops I had no intention of buying anything from. The whole while my eyes would be glued to Alice, waiting for her to speak again.

"Take me home."

It was a thought that served no purpose, of course. Alice couldn't speak. Her vocal cords had burned in the fire. They were the smoke that had risen from the house—the collective scream of hurt children rising silent and unnoticed into the sky.

Alice was all of us.

All that remained was likely her chains. I remembered the way they rattled against the basement concrete in the dead of night. It had been a comfort to me once. The sound of companionship without end.

I imagined her parents. What was their life like? Did they keep her room as it was when she was kidnapped? Did they really still hope she would return? Had her abduction caused a rift in their marriage? Could they even still love after losing her?

True Crime talked about the surviving relatives sometimes. It talked about how their lives changed forever, about how their marriages fell apart or how they committed suicide.

If I could've put the genie back in the bottle, I would've. I couldn't say I felt regret or even understood it, as it were, but I felt a sadness for little Alice. The same sadness I supposed I felt for all little things. We were waiting to be abused, all of us, abused into monsters or abused into ash. If there were someone who could have healed me—therapist, preacher, teacher, father—I never knew him.

Man always thought he could fix anything he saw. And what he couldn't fix, he sought to destroy.

I called Mr. Jack's on a whim. I had a flyer of Alice's face folded neatly in my pocket for safekeeping. She might say something to me later. She had all the secrets of the universe in her now. Did God exist? Was life just a long conveyor belt to dust? Did the little broken things like her have a special place in Heaven—whatever Heaven might be—where little broken things could sit side by side? Only Alice knew.

It would take more than Man to put Alice back together again.

I asked Mr. Jack if Milton were there, but Mr. Jack said he hadn't seen Milton in a few days. Hadn't heard from him, even. He asked why I was asking. I hung up without giving an answer.

The air buzzed around me. Alice whispered from my pocket but her words were too garbled to understand.

And everybody that passed me looked shameful, their curves of flesh an aberration of space. I wanted Lim to lean into, to look up at. I wanted to get lost in his small eyes and ask him all the questions I never did ask. I felt stupid then because even though I had seen death so closely, I always felt like Lim would live forever. I always felt like, one day, I'd have the chance to ask him if he loved me.

But what good was love, anyway? I felt the shape of the flyer in my pocket, gave it a caress. Alice was loved. Love never helped her. Love never helped anyone, did it? Love was a complication.

And yet, if I were to speak honestly, I could say I still wanted to know if Lim had loved me.

I got in the car. It was already dusk. If I headed over to Mr. Lorry's now, it would be nighttime by the time I arrived. I could tell him I had to run errands. I could tell him I overslept. There were so many ready lies.

Instead of going straight to the old man's house, I first stopped at the cathedral. Downtown was abuzz with the sort of men that made ill fathers. I saw some of them catcall the women who walked fast and afraid with crossbody purses clutched tight at the hip.

I walked with a sense of leisure. I made too much eye contact. I invited anyone to accost me. There was a sense of curiosity about what could be done that hadn't already been done. Flesh could only take so many forms.

I asked to see the monseigneur once inside and was told he was busy. I pulled out the crumpled flyer of Alice and held it up.

"It's important to some people," I said.

The volunteer gave me a quizzical look. "I'll see if he can make time," she said and scuttled off down the hall, though not without looking over her shoulder at me as she left.

When the monseigneur arrived, he looked tired. His usual charm seemed dimmed. I could tell he was vaguely annoyed at having his schedule interrupted, but he managed a smile nonetheless.

"Suzy, it's so good to see you!"

His eyes flitted to the flyer and then back to me. He looked at his volunteer. Concern was written all over her face. I figured she knew who I was.

"Margaret, you can leave us," he said. She seemed reluctant to go but there was no way for her to politely protest.

The monseigneur ushered me into his office.

There was a garishly large figure of an apostle, carved in white, on his desk. "A gift," he said, "for the baptism of the mayor's son." The monseigneur flashed a smile at me, teeth and all.

He gestured at the empty armchair, but he himself did not sit and so I also stood. We squared off against each other and I might've seen a flicker of fear pass through his charming eyes.

"What is it you need to tell me?"

I slid the flyer onto his desk and, though I urged Alice to speak for herself, I knew she could not. So I told him instead.

"It's not hard, you know," I began. "It's not hard to do right and it's not hard to do wrong. They're different sides of the same basketball court. You know?"

"Suzy . . ."

"I can't tell you how she got there. I came home from school one day and it was what it was."

"Got where?"

The monseigneur took an almost imperceptible step toward me. His feet seemed like they were itching to approach.

"Mama's basement. I left for school one day and it was empty, but when I came home, Alice was there."

"Are you saying your brother kidnapped Alice Gibbons? Do you know how long the family has been searching for her?"

I shrugged. It didn't seem important at this point to think about how long they'd been searching. The important thing was that she went home.

"In the first days, it was bad. It's not important to tell you about the first days. Don't tell her parents about that," I said. "But after a while, she got used to it alright. It wasn't Lim who took her. It was Mama. And it wasn't Lim who hurt her, either." My voice quaked a little at the last part.

"Where is she now?" he asked as he took another small step toward me.

I looked at the photo of Jesus Christ hanging above the monseigneur's desk. His somber eyes looked back at me from beneath his thorned crown.

"She's dead now. Anyway, that's all I wanted to tell you. So you can tell them." I gestured to the flyer where it mentioned Alice's parents and a contact number. "I can't change it. Neither can you." I pointed at the portrait of Jesus. "And neither can he."

I walked toward the door and the monseigneur held out a hand to stop me.

"Where are you going? The police will want to question you. This is a huge revelation . . ."

"I'm not answering any questions right now, but if you pin this on Lim, Monseigneur," I said and I smiled in my own way at him, "you'll get a chance to put your faith to the test."

I opened the door and started walking out of the cathedral.

The monseigneur called out about ten paces behind me, "Suzy!"

I turned around and looked at him.

"Before you go, at least tell me one thing."

His blue eyes held mine in the tension of anticipation.

"Were there other girls?" he asked.

"None that are missed," I replied.

I turned around and left the cathedral. I never looked back. Let him sit with his rosaries. Let him sit and pray. Alice prayed.

In those first days, she had prayed a lot.

25

IT FELT GOOD to have told someone about Alice. The monseigneur would know what to do with the information. After all, he was a holy man.

The drive to Mr. Lorry's was long and lonely. I thought about Lim again and what Milton had said about his time in prison. Was I the reason Lim was dead? I couldn't say I felt guilt over it, but it did confuse me. I wasn't worth Lim breaking someone's arm over and I never had been worth that much.

It was dark outside by the time I pulled up to Mr. Lorry's. Something was strange. I hadn't gone to the old man's house in a few days even though I had said I would. The porch light was off and I didn't hear the dogs barking. Usually at least Lachesis would come out to greet me.

The mosquitos were hungry tonight. They latched onto my skin and I didn't bother to swat them off. They could feed and flee as they pleased. I wondered which other men and animals they spit back into me.

I looked around the porch. It was hard to see in the dim moonlight. I waited for the dogs to start barking. I was wary they wouldn't know who I was in the dark and that they might attack me.

I walked the length of the porch. The porch slats creaked beneath my feet as I stepped. I squinted into the darkness to try to see where the German shepherds were. Were they sleeping? The sound of the car approaching would've been enough to wake them up, even if they had been inside.

Around the corner and off the porch, I finally saw the poor girl. She was huddled in a curled mass on the ground. It was what could only be the figure of a dog. I couldn't see which one it was but it wasn't moving. I approached it with trepidation. If she were sick, she might lash out at me.

As I approached, the smell caught me by surprise. And then I heard the buzzing whirl of the insect herd. It was one of the dogs—and it was rotting.

I kneeled next to her body and pressed my hand against her matted, fly-breeding fur. I then held up the same hand against the moonlight and saw the evidence of death. Her body was mutilated, but I surmised it was Lachesis from what I could see in the dark. She had been dead for a bit. Maybe a day, I figured.

"It took you awhile to come 'round," a voice said from behind me. I hadn't heard anyone approach and so the words had caught me by surprise. I leapt back in the darkness and faced the direction from where the sound had come.

It was Milton.

"Old man's got his shit hidden good," Milton said.

"What did you do with him?"

"Oh you care about that fucker, huh?" Milton laughed. "Well don't worry. He's alive."

Milton kicked the dog's corpse, "His dogs aren't, though. Fucking mutt stinks like shit."

I was surprised the dogs hadn't killed Milton. They were protective and beautiful. But Milton was a career criminal and the way I figured it to myself, he was a bit of a specialist at his job. It was like when you called the bug man around. You saw something crawling up your walls at night and you didn't know how to get rid of it, but the bug man did. Such was with Milton and anything living. He may have been blunt and brutish, but he had experience in the only way of life he'd ever tried.

"Here, I tell you what," Milton said, "you suck my cock right here and I'll promise not to kill the old fuck." Milton laughed again.

"Where is he?" I asked.

"Inside. What's left of him anyhow. Still got breath so he's still got life."

"So they say," I said.

"So how about it? It ain't like I gotta ask, really, but I'm trying to be nice." I thought I saw his teeth in the moonlight.

A ragged scream howled from inside the house. It was Mr. Lorry alright. It couldn't have been anyone else.

I sized Milton up. I couldn't see both of his hands and so I didn't know what he had in store for me or had been dishing out to Mr. Lorry.

The screaming continued from inside the house. It sounded pained and pleading. Like the screaming of a wounded thing that couldn't stop if it tried, the pain was too much. I'd heard that kind of screaming before.

"You can't save him. Not unless you do what I want," Milton said. He casually leaned against one of the porch's pillars. His slanting figure with the rotting shepherd in the foreground made an impression.

"I'm not interested in saving him," I said. "And I'm not interested in sucking your cock either."

I kicked the shepherd's corpse myself. A group of flies lifted off it and buzzed briefly in front of my face before dropping to feed again. Mixed in between the sound of Mr. Lorry's screams was a whole orchestral symphony of insects, both flying and crawling around us.

"I only came to say goodbye and I guess this is as good as any."

"So you don't care about him, huh? Were just fucking him for the money?"

I laughed at the notion. "There's no money. I told you there's no money. And what does it matter if I care? That gonna change your mind? Me caring?"

I knew caring never changed a bad man's mind. Just excited it, was all. I wouldn't give him any satisfaction.

I headed toward my car. I expected Milton to attack me from

behind. I knew it would probably be a lost cause if he did. I was tired and sure he was armed with something.

But he didn't attack or pursue me. He laughed the whole time while I walked. His laughter was a constant track to the music of the night: Mr. Lorry's screams, the buzz of devouring flies, and Milton's unfiltered joy.

I hoped he would let Mr. Lorry live, but at the same time, I couldn't say I really cared one way or the other. Mr Lorry had probably taught me all he was going to teach me and, besides, he was a good man. If goodness had purpose or existed at all, then good would be rewarded in the end. My hand didn't have to sway it one way or the other.

I got in my car and revved the engine. I turned on the headlights and saw Milton still leaning against the porch's pillar. He had a knife in his hand he stroked with the other in the light of my high beams. He smiled.

To each their own.

I drove off Mr. Lorry's property with my head aflame with troubled thoughts. I'd probably never know for sure why Milton let me leave, but I suspected he wasn't that excited by my nonchalance for the whole affair.

I felt bad for Mr. Lorry. I really did. And I felt even worse for the dogs. They were beautiful.

I knew how to get to the highway that headed west and that's where I was going. I knew there was a timer that had started as soon as I'd told the monseigneur about Alice. I knew they were looking for me.

Then again, they were always looking for me. People like me. My kind.

I stopped at a lonely country gas station. It had two pumps and you had to pay inside. The small store was flooded with fluorescent light. The cashier was a young kid—maybe fifteen or sixteen years old—and he wore a t-shirt with Lim's face on the front. Lim's eyes in the print were cold but they didn't capture the chill his gaze had in real life. There wasn't a way for any reproduction or photo to capture that feeling.

I handed over some cash and nodded my head in the direction of the window. "Put it all on pump one."

The kid nodded and sorted the bills into their appropriate slots.

"Do you need a receipt?"

"No, but—tell me. Is that man on your shirt Lim—?"

"Yeah!" he said with enthusiasm. His dour work-bored face changed suddenly into one of excitement. "Do you know about him? I love these guys. Serial killers, I mean. I love reading about them. They're so weird and creepy. Can you imagine what it would be like to live with one?"

I stared at him for a long moment before answering. "Why are you wearing a t-shirt with his face?"

The kid shrugged. His excitement began to wane as soon as he saw I wasn't as enthusiastic as he was. "Just kinda cool, I guess. He killed a lot of people."

I nodded. He was a dumb kid. A young kid. A safe kid.

"You take care now," I said and I walked out to fill my car.

As I pumped gas into the tank, I saw the kid ogle his own shirt inside the store. He then looked out at me and quickly looked away when we made brief eye contact.

I left the gas station and headed into the night as Lim and I once had together. I drove toward the highway and thought of what I'd have to do to survive. I thought of my next meal. And thought of how I was going to get my next meal.

I thought of Mr. Lorry, too.

And Alice.

And Lena.

And Mama.

I thought of them all. And I realized I could've saved any one of them.

But I wasn't a Builder. I wasn't a Creator. I was a maggot, like Mr. Lorry had said. And I knew other maggots like Milton. And though we couldn't make anything beautiful, we did know how to feed and multiply.

I was one of a teeming mass spread out over the vast country. We wriggled our ways and spread our pain everywhere we were spotted, an infestation of the open road.

An infestation that teenagers celebrated and publishers craved. An infestation that made newscasters lick their lips. Over dinner, they relished the details of every last criminal act. They said it repulsed them, but it never stopped them from eating dessert.

I drove the roads at night thinking about the next meal. I'd killed for a meal before. I'd killed for less and I'd killed for more.

It was sad that Lim was gone.

As an idea, it was sad.

But I'd never needed him anyway.

At least not any more than a carpenter needed a hammer.

And I could always find a new hammer.

Acknowledgments

Great thanks are owed to author C.V. Hunt and Grindhouse Press for giving this book a home. Thank you to Mike Lombardo and Brian Keene for their support. Additional thanks to Andersen Prunty for his editing prowess. Lastly, thank you to all of my friends, past and present.

Samantha Kolesnik is an award-winning writer and film director living in central Pennsylvania. Her screenplays and short films have been recognized at top genre film festivals and her fiction has appeared in notable literary magazines including *The Bitter Oleander*, *The William and Mary Review*, and *Barnstorm*. She is one of the co-founders of the Women in Horror Film Festival. *True Crime* is her first novel.

Other Grindhouse Press Titles

#666__*Satanic Summer* by Andersen Prunty
#057__*The Cycle* by John Wayne Comunale
#056__*A Voice So Soft* by Patrick Lacey
#055__*Merciless* by Bryan Smith
#054__*The Long Shadows of October* by Kristopher Triana
#053__*House of Blood* by Bryan Smith
#052__*The Freakshow* by Bryan Smith
#051__*Dirty Rotten Hippies and Other Stories* by Bryan Smith
#050__*Rites of Extinction* by Matt Serafini
#049__*Saint Sadist* by Lucas Mangum
#048__*Neon Dies at Dawn* by Andersen Prunty
#047__*Halloween Fiend* by C.V. Hunt
#046__*Limbs: A Love Story* by Tim Meyer
#045__*As Seen On T.V.* by John Wayne Comunale
#044__*Where Stars Won't Shine* by Patrick Lacey
#043__*Kinfolk* by Matt Kurtz
#042__*Kill For Satan!* by Bryan Smith
#041__*Dead Stripper Storage* by Bryan Smith
#040__*Triple Axe* by Scott Cole
#039__*Scummer* by John Wayne Comunale
#038__*Cockblock* by C.V. Hunt
#037__*Irrationalia* by Andersen Prunty
#036__*Full Brutal* by Kristopher Triana
#035__*Office Mutant* by Pete Risley
#034__*Death Pacts and Left-Hand Paths* by John Wayne Comunale
#033__*Home Is Where the Horror Is* by C.V. Hunt
#032__*This Town Needs A Monster* by Andersen Prunty
#031__*The Fetishists* by A.S. Coomer
#030__*Ritualistic Human Sacrifice* by C.V. Hunt
#029__*The Atrocity Vendor* by Nick Cato

#028__*Burn Down the House and Everyone In It* by Zachary T. Owen
#027__*Misery and Death and Everything Depressing* by C.V. Hunt
#026__*Naked Friends* by Justin Grimbol
#025__*Ghost Chant* by Gina Ranalli
#024__*Hearers of the Constant Hum* by William Pauley III
#023__*Hell's Waiting Room* by C.V. Hunt
#022__*Creep House: Horror Stories* by Andersen Prunty
#021__*Other People's Shit* by C.V. Hunt
#020__*The Party Lords* by Justin Grimbol
#019__*Sociopaths In Love* by Andersen Prunty
#018__*The Last Porno Theater* by Nick Cato
#017__*Zombieville* by C.V. Hunt
#016__*Samurai Vs. Robo-Dick* by Steve Lowe
#015__*The Warm Glow of Happy Homes* by Andersen Prunty
#014__*How To Kill Yourself* by C.V. Hunt
#013__*Bury the Children in the Yard: Horror Stories* by Andersen Prunty
#012__*Return to Devil Town (Vampires in Devil Town Book Three)* by Wayne Hixon
#011__*Pray You Die Alone: Horror Stories* by Andersen Prunty
#010__*King of the Perverts* by Steve Lowe
#009__*Sunruined: Horror Stories* by Andersen Prunty
#008__*Bright Black Moon (Vampires in Devil Town Book Two)* by Wayne Hixon
#007__*Hi I'm a Social Disease: Horror Stories* by Andersen Prunty
#006__*A Life On Fire* by Chris Bowsman
#005__*The Sorrow King* by Andersen Prunty
#004__*The Brothers Crunk* by William Pauley III
#003__*The Horribles* by Nathaniel Lambert
#002__*Vampires in Devil Town* by Wayne Hixon
#001__*House of Fallen Trees* by Gina Ranalli
#000__*Morning is Dead* by Andersen Prunty

CPSIA information can be obtained
at www.ICGtesting.com
Printed in the USA
FSHW021025120620
71133FS